Our Brave Star

THE LOST STAR TRILOGY: BOOK ONE

JESSI LANIER

ISBN 978-1-64258-656-5 (paperback)
ISBN 978-1-64258-657-2 (digital)

Christian Faith Publishing, Inc.
832 Park Avenue
Meadville, PA 16335
www.christianfaithpublishing.com

Printed in the United States of America

I would like to dedicate this book to my mom. Mom, you are the reason that I have the inherited God-given talent to write. Your passion for writing was infectious, and I couldn't help but love to read and write from a very young age. You always encouraged and motivated me to perfect my writing and to always tell a good story. You edited my stories and helped me do the best I could. You and Dad sent me to a Christian school for most of my life and made sacrifices so I could get a strong foundation on Christ. You showed me how to be a preacher's wife, which I never thought I would need to know, but it has come in handy! You showed me how to be a supportive mother and friend to my children. Thanks, Mom, for being my biggest fan and believing I could write. This story is for you.

To my husband and kids—Trey, Hannah, and Luke you have all been so amazing in supporting me in my writing and have helped me tremendously by your encouragement, love, and laughter.

Finally, I dedicate this book to all Jews, Jewish families, and *all* the victims of the Holocaust, no matter the race. Also, to all the survivors and all those who were affected by this horrific time in history. God has chosen you to be His people and He has a plan for each of you. You are remembered, honored, and dearly missed. May we never forget.

CHAPTER 1

The Day It All Began

"I just don't understand why you have to go back to the office. I can't understand why you are never home anymore. The kids need their father, Alex."

"Liz, I have already told you, I need to get my papers that were faxed from the insurance company. Corporate is hounding us to push the deadline up."

"I guess your work takes priority again over your family."

"My job pays the bills in this house, and I would appreciate it if you would recognize and respect that instead of criticize and condescend!"

Her dad's voice was rising again and she could hear the emotion her mom was trying to hold back. "Why do they always have to fight like this?" Hannah asked herself. She heard a pause and then the door slam as her dad no doubt marched out of the house and headed to his black beat-up Chevy pickup truck. At least Charlie, her younger brother, was at a neighbor's house playing basketball and missed this fight. The yelling seemed to be all her parents did nowadays. They couldn't be in a room together for long and anyone could feel the tension. Hannah knew it was only a matter of days before her parents sat her, Charlie, and their older sister, Beth, down for "the talk." She wanted so bad for her parents to kiss and make up, but she felt in her gut that would never happen. There was too much said, the damage done.

Oh well, she had to focus on her mound of homework or she would never be able to pass her English class. *I don't know why Mrs. Lannister insisted I take this Honors English class in the first place?* Hannah questioned to herself. *I don't have time for all the loads of work the teachers pile on us. This year I want to focus on playing volleyball and try out for cheer.* She looked over at the full-length mirror on the wall behind her closet door. Her nutmeg-brown hair fell in loose waves just below her shoulders. Hazel-green eyes stared back at her with a grim expression of sadness.

After mentally listing all the reasons why she didn't want to focus on the world and all the chaos that ensued under Hitler's rule in Europe in the early 1940s, she finally settled her mind enough to read the first chapter in the assigned novel, *The Holocaust: Fact or fiction?*

When her head began to ache and her eyes felt tense, Hannah quickly left her book on her bed with a bookmark securing her spot in chapter two and headed to see if her mom needed help with supper. She found her mom in the kitchen stirring something in a pot on the stove. She looked up at Hannah and unshed tears made her eyes glisten.

"Beth called earlier and said she was staying at the dorm this evening to study for her calculus test so she won't be home till tomorrow or Saturday," Liz said sadly to her middle child.

"I'm sure we will see her as soon as she needs laundry done," Hannah stated sarcastically.

Beth was the "smart child" in the family. Beth had a gorgeous smile, shiny brown hair, and clear blue eyes. Their little brother, Charlie, was the "athletic one." Charlie was in eighth grade and at thirteen years old, he already towered over Hannah who was two years older than him. Hannah wasn't sure what she was or how she fit into her family. An inconvenience is what she felt like. She noticed her mother's casual stare out the window behind the kitchen sink overlooking the neighborhood.

"I hope your brother knows supper is about to be ready. He would stay outside playing ball all evening if his grumbling stomach would allow him to," her mom stated with a hint of a smile in her voice.

Hannah looked at her mom. In her midforties, she was a beautiful woman with auburn hair and green eyes. Her mom had a sweet smile. *Mom should smile more*, Hannah thought. *Maybe if Dad were home more during the day, then she would.*

"Will Dad be home for supper?" Charlie asked their mom later that evening, as the three of them sat down to beef stew and vegetables. Charlie's dirty blond hair was still wet from a shower, and he looked sheepishly at Hannah to see if he had said the wrong thing. Charlie was always concerned about others and wanted to please everyone he knew. Everyone, that is, but his two sisters. He loved to mercilessly joke and kid around with the two girls. She couldn't blame him though, he was the only boy in the house other than their dad, who was never home it seemed. Poor Charlie was highly outnumbered.

"Dad will be here soon," Mom said with a slight smile. "He had to run back to the office for some papers. I expect him any time now, but the stew is getting cold, so let's eat and I will keep it warm on the stove for him."

A half hour later, Hannah was done eating and helping clear away dishes when the phone rang. "Hello?" Hannah answered cautiously.

"Hey, girl." Hannah heard the familiar sound of her best friend, Riley's voice on the other end of the line.

She relaxed. "Hi. What are you up to this evening?" Hannah asked her friend.

"Well, I am trying to make myself read to chapter four in this novel for english class. How far have you gotten?" Riley questioned.

Before Hannah could answer, her dad breezed in the door, as if he had not a care in the world. Hannah was standing at the kitchen phone and turned her back on her parents as her mom silently made a bowl of stew and plate of cornbread for her dad. Wow, she could feel the tension between her parents.

Hannah finally responded, "Yeah, I need to go finish my reading for school tomorrow. I am so glad tomorrow is Friday. I really don't understand why we must study this stuff. I mean, do you even believe the Holocaust really happened? This Hitler guy couldn't have been as bad as he seems. There is no way countries would stand by while six million Jews were killed. It is inhumane. It bores me personally. Oh well, do you think Mrs. Lannister will give us a quiz on the vocabulary in chapters one to three tomorrow?"

"Who knows?" Riley responded. "Mrs. L. is known for giving pop quizzes on Fridays, so I wouldn't be surprised. I kind of find this history interesting. I mean, there is proof the concentration camps were real if you go over to Germany and other countries in Europe and see them."

"Yeah, like that will ever happen in my lifetime. Okay, well, I have got to go get busy on my homework," Hannah resolved. "I will see you in the morning." She hung up and quietly made her way down the hallway and up the stairs to her room. Once in her room, she shut her door softly, sat down with a graceful slide onto her bed, brushed her hair behind one ear, and stared at her novel. The girl on the cover had a plain, sad expression on her face. She saw determination for survival in her eyes.

"If only I could be in a different place. In a different time, even. These people in this book don't seem to have it so bad in my opinion. I would love to visit Europe. Maybe not back when a crazy dictator was in charge, but maybe when I graduate, I can backpack through Europe and maybe even intern for a semester of college in an orphanage in Europe! I would sure like to see these concentration camps to prove to myself this actually occurred or that they never even existed for that matter."

As Hannah began to read, she yawned. She didn't dare look at the clock, but she knew it had to be around 8:00 p.m. "Two more hours before Mom or Dad knocks on my bedroom door and then it's lights out for the night." She got up from the bed and put on her favorite pair of pajamas. They were light pink with flowers all over the shirt and pants. She topped them off with her warm, rose-colored robe and climbed back onto the bed to begin reading.

Suddenly, everything was dark except a bright light in the distance. "Shh," the voice of an unfamiliar girl whispered to Hannah.

"We can't make a sound or they will hear us." Hannah looked around at the small room she and this girl were crowded in. "Who will hear us?" She heard herself say barely above a whisper.

"The Nazi soldiers," the girl whispered back. "They are coming for us."

CHAPTER 2

The Hidden Room Behind a Bookshop in Amsterdam

"Where am I?" Hannah panicked. "This can't be happening. I am at home in my bedroom. Who is this girl? Why is it so dark in here?" Hannah blinked several times as she tried to adjust her eyes to the darkness. She realized a musty smell hung in the air and she felt damp with a chill. The girl beside her sat perfectly still. She could not even hear her breathing. Hannah peered through what looked like a small hole in the wall and she looked out into a bright room that seemed like a library or bookstore. Beyond that was a street lined with soldiers in uniforms. She mentally assessed her situation, trying not to panic.

Suddenly, she heard a chime of a bell above the door entrance to the bookshop. Her peephole was blocked with what appeared to be a gray uniform of one of the soldiers. "I swear, Lieutenant, I saw someone come in here," a gruff male voice said.

"Sergeant, I do not have time for this. This whole area was cleared weeks ago and the Jews taken to a ghetto. No one could have possibly come in here."

"I'd still feel better if you allowed me to search the rooms."

"It's a waste of time, I tell you. Let's move the men on down the corner."

Footsteps and the chime again indicated the soldiers had abandoned the store.

"Whew, that was a close one. Okay," the girl beside her said after what seemed like hours, but in reality, was only a few minutes. "I think they are gone."

"Who is gone?" Hannah asked.

"Those Nazi soldiers. We don't usually see them in this side of town at this time of day. Lucky for you, my papa saw you on the street in front of our bookshop, and he brought you into our hiding place before the soldiers caught you," the girl said. "We will wait a few more minutes before we move."

Hannah was trying her very best not to completely freak out. She found her voice and asked the question she knew she needed to know, but hoped she didn't come across as crazy. "Who are you and where are we?" Before the girl could answer, Hannah became aware they were not alone in the room and others were crouched down also on the damp floor. Two other children, younger than the girls, and a man who Hannah couldn't see well due to the darkness of their confined hiding space.

The girl began to speak to Hannah in what she just realized was a strange accent. "My name is Adelaide Dressler. You don't know where we are? We are in my papa's bookshop in Amsterdam, Netherlands."

Hannah's heart stopped. *What? How is this possible? Nazi soldiers in 2016? I must be dreaming!* she thought. Panic again began to rise in her throat and her heart raced wildly.

"What 'dis your name?" the girl asked in a thick accent that Hannah now realized was maybe Dutch-German.

Hannah's brain began to function after a beat and she knew her first name was okay for a Jew, but her last name, Johnson, would never be believable here. She remembered her Jewish roots on her mother's side of the family and decided to use her grandmother's maiden name as her own last name. She recovered some and could answer after a moment. "Hannah. My name is Hannah Rosenbaum." *There, that wasn't so hard, right?* she wondered.

"Hannah. I like that name. It is a strong Jewish name that dates back to biblical times. Hannah was 'favored of God,'" Adelaide said with awe and reverence.

She didn't know that about her name. Hannah always thought her name meant "grace." She couldn't even feel her chest rise and fall, but she knew she must be breathing. How was this even possible? A few minutes ago she was in her room reading and now she was in Europe hiding from Nazi soldiers? Nazis meant Hitler's soldiers. The Holocaust? How could she be smack-dab in the middle of the Holocaust? This must be a dream. There was no way she could be here. She pinched herself hard to try and wake up. The other people in the room with them were starting to move about and Hannah realized this couldn't be a dream, could it? She looked back through the hole and realized the sun was setting, and soon it would be dark.

"What day is it?" Hannah asked Adelaide.

"Thursday, January 6."

"This may sound crazy, but what year is it?" Hannah asked slowly.

"Why, it is 1942, of course," Adelaide responded with a somewhat sad tone.

"Whoa, 1942? Impossible!" Hannah spouted off without realizing what she had done.

"Yes," Adelaide stated sadly. "It is unbelievable, isn't it? That we have been in hiding from this German monster and his soldiers for almost three years now."

Hannah felt her stomach form knots and then take a nosedive. "Three years of hiding?" She couldn't even fathom this. She turned and realized her eyes were adjusting better. Soon an oil lamp was lit, and the room became more real to her. The others all turned and as a trapdoor was unlocked, they began to make their way down a creaking staircase to what appeared to be a basement. Hannah obediently followed the others to what opened up to be a great hidden room. Several other people were there already and she began to wonder what she was about to learn from them. Small candles were lit and another oil lamp was also lit to provide enough light to see all around her. There were a few pieces of broken furniture, some scraps of food, books scattered, makeshift cots, and blankets strewn throughout.

"So you live down here?" Hannah couldn't help but ask her new friend.

Adelaide sighed and smiled slightly. "Yes. We have been down here for two years. My family and another one as well. We are having to hide from the Nazi soldiers because we are all Jews. The Germans boycotted all Jewish businesses here in Amsterdam in March of 1939, closing our bookshop, but Papa, however, was able to continue to teach at the school until a little over three years ago when the soldiers invaded this area. For now, there is no more school," she stated solemnly.

"No school? That doesn't sound so bad to me," Hannah said absently. She quickly realized how rude that must have sounded. "I am sorry. I didn't mean to be unkind. I am not too thrilled with my school classes is all I meant."

"Where are you from, Hannah? You obviously are not from Amsterdam. Your accent is unfamiliar to me," Adelaide shyly questioned.

Hannah paused and tried to remember her weak European geography knowledge. She couldn't admit she was from the United States. New Hampshire, to be exact, born in 2001. They would all think she was delusional. She was, though, and this had to be a dream. It had to be. Things like this didn't happen. It was all made up in books. Hitler wasn't as evil as everyone implied in books, was he?

"Hannah, where did you go just now? I just wondered from where do you come?" Adelaide asked her. "You don't have to be afraid, you can tell me where you are from. I am also a Jew. Dutch-German, to be exact. I am originally from a small area close to Auschwitz, Germany. When Hitler rose to power several years ago, and the Jews became a threat to him, my family moved here to Amsterdam to escape him and his soldiers. We got a nice house in the garden district. My papa opened this bookshop and also taught at the local school until it was all shutdown by the invading soldiers. Then, we had to leave our new house and go into hiding."

"Wow. That is unbelievable. Your family has been forced into hiding because of all this? That seems unreal. What would the soldiers do to you all if they caught you?"

"Just what they do to all Jews. Send them to the ghettos and eventually back to Auschwitz to the German concentration camps. They call it 'relocation.'"

"Concentration camps? I have heard of those. They really do exist?" Hannah asked unbelievably.

"Oh yes, they do exist and they are as deadly as their reputation. Once on our journey here, we could smell the burning and see the smoke. That is not something I will ever forget." Adelaide shuttered at the memory.

"So, I am from Denmark," Hannah blurted out the first country name that came to her.

"Oh, yes, that explains the fact that you aren't wearing your badge."

"Badge?" Hannah asked.

"The yellow star of David. All Jews must wear a badge. It looks different in each country, but I wondered why you weren't wearing yours. I learned from papa that Denmark didn't require badges under King Christian X's rule."

Hannah looked down at that moment and realized she was not in her robe and pajamas, but in jeans and a red shirt with a denim jacket. The very outfit she had worn earlier that day at home. *How odd*, she thought. She looked around at the other people gathered in the room with them and realized they had been inconspicuously listening to their whole conversation. Somehow, she didn't feel strange among these people. They had a kind way about them. She was about to inquire as to everyone's names knowing she would probably forget them, but Adelaide interrupted her.

"Hannah, I have an extra cot and blanket I will share with you. We should sleep. You look exhausted and confused."

"I am," Hannah admitted to both.

The girls laid down on side by side cots, and before she knew what was happening, Hannah fell into a deep sleep.

CHAPTER 3

The Dressler's Make a New Ally

"Hannah, Hannah, wake up."

She heard a somewhat familiar voice of a girl calling to her. She blinked and opened her eyes to reveal that she was in a strange room lit by candles and oil lamps. It was so damp in there with a chill in the air. "Was she dreaming or was this really happening?"

"Morning, Hannah. It is almost daylight and time for us to wake up."

"Ugh," Hannah groaned. She sat up and quickly realized that a tall, slender boy with wavy, brown hair and the most handsome face she had ever seen was sitting in a corner wearing a strange uniform. Adelaide followed her gaze.

"Oh, that's my brother, Seth. He is part of the Resistance."

"Resistance?" Hannah was confused and embarrassed at the same time.

Seth spoke to her then. "The Resistance is a group of Jewish teens and young adults who are part of an uprising against Hitler and his pig-headed German soldiers. We bring food to Jewish families in hiding to make and set off bombs to destroy the German's railroad track system transporting people to concentration camps and many other things Hitler has set to transport."

Hannah could hardly breathe. She was captivated by this boy and the cause for which he stood to lose everything, including his life. She felt sadness and an overwhelming feeling she couldn't quite place.

Adelaide then introduced Hannah to her two little sisters, Gretchen and Liesel. Gretchen had dirty brown hair that hung straight past her shoulders and little Liesel had brown curls that fell to her chin, framing her heart-shaped face. Hannah learned that Seth, at seventeen years old, was the eldest Dressler sibling. Adelaide was fourteen years old, Gretchen was ten, and Liesel was seven. Hannah fell in love with them all immediately. Meeting them officially made her homesick for her own siblings. She looked down into the haunted, brown eyes of little Liesel and almost cried. "What struggles could this little girl have experienced in her short lifetime?" Hannah wondered.

"Where are your family, Hannah?" Gretchen asked cautiously.

After pondering for a moment, she answered honestly, "I'm not sure anymore."

The Dressler mother, Greta, a plump woman with a kind face interrupted, "Well, dear, you are welcome to stay here as long as you need. However, we should go over the rules with you."

Hannah sat up, fully awake now, and for the first time, she felt a little scared for her own life. She had not even thought about the fact that her own Jewish name and the fact that she was hiding in a strange place with Jews, put her own life at risk.

"First off, we need to give you another name to use in case you are ever caught. Let's see, Hannah is beautiful, but your death sentence, I'm afraid, if we are going to continue to be German-occupied here in Amsterdam. Hmm. What about Kate or Katie?"

Hannah thought for a moment and she liked the sound of that. She could be a Katie for now. She wasn't quite sure she still wasn't dreaming this whole thing, but seemed more convinced of its reality when Adelaide touched her arm and said sincerely, "Katie is a pretty name."

"Okay," Mrs. Dressler continued. "Now, that we have your new name established, let's go over some ground rules. You are not to ever go outside the bookshop during the day. It is far too risky. You are a beautiful young lady and new here, and the soldiers will be all too interested in who you are."

"Mother," Seth interrupted, "we could use Katie to help us with the Resistance. If she was willing to run some errands a few nights ..."

"Absolutely not, it is far too dangerous," Mrs. Dressler answered for her.

Hannah spoke up. "Look, I want to help you all. I am just not from here, so I know where nothing is and how to go about the city. I am, however, a fast learner." She stopped to take a breath.

"We start teaching you tonight then. It is almost dawn and I must sneak out. Mother, I have brought enough provisions for you for a few days. I wasn't planning to come back, but I will see what I can do to sneak by late tonight and teach Hannah, I mean Katie, a few things. She really could be useful to our cause."

Hannah looked from Seth to Mrs. Dressler then to Adelaide who sat with a tight smile on her lips. Mrs. Dressler said to him, "Okay, Seth. I love you, please be careful." With a tight hug from his mother, Seth vanished up the stairs.

Hannah sat beside Adelaide and as they munched on a piece of stale bread shaped like a biscuit and drank murky water, she asked her new friend many questions about the Resistance and the Nazis. Hannah became fascinated with the Jews and how they were the definition of survival. She had no idea Hitler was so vicious. Her thoughts were racing through her head. "He really is as evil as I have read. I just always thought that stuff was fictional and made up for entertaining purposes. He really is setting out to massacre every Jew he can." Hannah wasn't sure now how to process this new revelation, but she knew one thing for sure. She had to do whatever she could to help her new friends, even if it meant putting her own life in danger.

CHAPTER 4

Choices and Consequences

Hannah spent the rest of the day engrossed in conversation with the other members of their hiding place. She found the children's stories fascinating. She was captivated by these Jews and what they had experienced in their lives. She began to realize how much the history books were correct about this time in history. She never would have thought people could be so cruel to other human beings. She learned that the Jews were to be "dehumanized or set apart" from all other races and looked down upon by many. She remembered studying one time in her Sunday school class about how Jesus was a Jew and even though she didn't pay much attention to what her teacher had said at the time, she did catch that much to be a fact in the Bible.

Gretchen spoke up the most those first few days. She told of fascinating stories when the Dressler family had almost been captured by the German soldiers. They were helping their relatives escape a transport leaving for Warsaw, Poland, where it was rumored there was a ghetto established to separate and house Jews before sending them off to concentration camps. Gretchen excitedly told Hannah, "We just barely escaped from being discovered in the woods by Nazi soldiers. They had these mean dogs with them that were trained to kill. They growled and barked if they smelled a human. Their bark is something I will never forget. If it hadn't been for Seth, we would have been captured. I just know it. He caused a diversion by exploding a barrel of gunpowder, and the soldiers all took off for the commotion. That gave us a small window of opportunity to escape through the path in the woods. We made it back here safely, but it was so close!"

Hannah's head was spinning by the time the hidden group began to breathe without fear that evening. The day seemed to be tense and restless. Her eyes ached from being in a dimly-lit room all day.

"Are things always so tense around here during the day?" Hannah asked Gretchen as they sat by a lamp drawing pictures of flowers and trees in a meadow on a small drawing pad Gretchen treasured.

"Yes, Katie," Gretchen replied with a melancholic expression in her soft brown eyes. "Things lately are always tense and we never know when we may be discovered and taken away to the places we don't dare to speak of."

"Oh," Hannah stated flatly. She thought she must be referring to the concentration camps. German soldiers were stalking back and forth down the streets all day out in front of the bookshop and they would stop and interrogate anyone they felt like was in violation of their statutes. This was information Hannah learned from one of the other male adults who were also sharing this small hideout. She learned the other family were the Kern family. Mr. Kern spent all day with Mr. Dressler in another area of the bookshop, concealed, she was quite sure of. Not one of them could risk being captured. She curiously wondered what the men did all day there in the bookshop.

Mrs. Kern had suspicious, shifting eyes that darted all about the room. She made Hannah quite nervous if she watched her much at all. Hannah feared that Mrs. Kern may scream out loud and give them all away at any moment. She seemed to be out of her mind unless Mrs. Dressler or her children spoke softly to her, which seemed to calm the woman down. She had four small children. Every Kern child seemed pleasant, but they were very quiet and kept to themselves, playing a small makeshift board game on the dirty floor. One of the Kern children had a terrible cough. It wasn't loud, but seemed to be difficult for the child.

Hannah felt so sorry for these poor children who had to spend their years living this way. She thought of her own childhood and the wonderful times she had playing with the neighborhood kids and her own brother and sister. They would be outside from the time breakfast ended until sunset. They knew to be home by dark or their momma would be calling for them to come inside. These poor children would never understand what a wonderful time they could have if their lives would just be different. They needed to escape from here and be free.

Hannah wanted so bad to tell her own childhood stories to the children when Gretchen asked about her family numerous times during that day, but of course, she couldn't do that for two reasons. First, it would give away who she really was, and from where she came. Second, she did not want to make any of them feel bad for not being able to experience a truly amazing childhood. She wondered if these kids had any truly wonderful memories at all. Just then, a noise at the door made everyone's breathing stop. Whew, it was just Mr. Dressler and Mr. Kern coming in, with Seth at their heels.

They all said a strange prayer that Hannah assumed was Jewish custom. They had done that this morning and at midday as well. She bowed her head and closed her eyes. She didn't speak but listened intently. She wondered, *These people were hiding for their lives, and yet they took the time to pray three times today?* Hannah didn't even begin to understand that kind of faith. She reasoned to herself, *I mean, sure, I went to church growing up. We would go on Sunday mornings when my parents felt like it, which wasn't often here lately.* Thinking about her parents made Hannah sad and strangely ache for her own home. She hoped her parents were getting along and not worrying about where she was right now. They were probably arguing now ...

Hannah turned to her friend, Adelaide, and noticed for the first time that she wore a necklace with a star around her neck. "It was a gift from my grandmother to my mother, and now it has been passed down to me," Adelaide interrupted her thoughts, answering the question in Hannah's eyes. Hannah reached out to touch the necklace. The chain was simply a black thin cord of rope and the star was a dull titanium finished Star of David. In its simplicity, it was the most beautiful thing Hannah had ever seen. "It is so perfect." That was all she could think to say, and reached her right index finger to touch it. Adelaide smiled and their friendship was officially sealed.

Seth came to sit down beside her, and as they ate a small meal of bread and cheese with a strong drink that Hannah assumed was wine, he spoke to her and to Adelaide about the Resistance and their new mission to destroy a piece of the railroad track three miles down the road that was rumored to have a train coming in carrying supplies to the German Nazi soldiers. They also had plans to raid a supply wagon that was already stationed in Amsterdam's very public park a few blocks from the bookshop. The Resistance group consisted of mostly boys and a few older teenage Jewish girls, who were brave enough to risk their lives to take down the Nazi occupation in the Netherlands.

If Hannah admitted to herself her true feelings, she was terrified to even be thinking about rising with these people against the Germans, but she felt a thrill of excitement at the prospect of helping. She looked at Adelaide and she noticed a hint of glimmer in her eyes. She wanted desperately to help, but their father forbade it until she was at least sixteen years old. "It is far too dangerous for a young girl to partake in these endeavors." She overheard Mr. Dressler warn them. "I can't stop Seth, but I can forbid Adelaide to participate in a suicide mission."

"Suicide mission!" Hannah's thoughts of reason screamed at her to wake up from this nightmare, but she didn't and she knew she couldn't. She had to help them. She cautiously asked Seth how she could help.

"Well, I spoke to one of our leaders and we need a spy to keep a lookout at the corner, facing the supply wagon. We would need to come up with a signal for you to let us know if any Nazi soldiers were to come that way and then conceal yourself without getting caught." He made it sound so simple, but Hannah knew it would be anything but simple. What if she were caught by a soldier? What if they mistook her for a Jew? She was, after all, the great-granddaughter of a Jew from this exact time era. A young girl herself back then, who escaped Hitler and made a journey by ship to America from Sweden, after being smuggled across the sea from Denmark before the havoc unfolded in 1938. Hannah concentrated on her thoughts. "What was that story her mother had told her about her great-grandmother being smuggled through Denmark to Sweden by a boat? Something about a handkerchief laced with a substance to deter the soldier's dogs. What was it? Cocaine, I think? Man, I should have listened closely to mom's stories." She never really believed it was anything other than a silly story her mom had told her growing up. Now, however, she realized how true this all was and the very dangerous consequences that lurked around every corner.

CHAPTER 5

The Resistance: Mission Accomplished!

"This is Katie. She is here to help us with the mission tonight. If anyone has a concern for us to share before we head out, then speak now. This is probably one of the most dangerous missions we have had. Soldiers are standing on the street corner of Amstel and Damrak. The wagon with the supplies is surrounded by guards and nestled in a corner of a covered area north of Damrak Plaza. We should keep very quiet and out of sight until the shift rotation occurs. We have been keeping an eye on the shift rotations and feel that the best time to strike is at zero two hundred fifteen hours. If Katie sees a soldier headed our way, she will use this flashlight to signal us. One flash per number of soldiers. Got it?"

It was clear to her from the beginning of the evening that Seth was the humble leader of this Resistance group. She was told there were other groups in other German-occupied countries. Seth handed her the flashlight he had stolen from a soldier's bag earlier that day, and she nodded her head to indicate she understood her role. Everyone also nodded and the plan was set into motion.

A few minutes later, Hannah was nervously chewing on her left thumbnail. She hated when she did this, but she couldn't seem to break the nervous habit. How did she get here? Right smack dab in the middle of a covert operation in Amsterdam during the Holocaust? "This must be some bizarre story I've found myself in." She tried to reason to herself. The sound of approaching soldiers jolted her back to reality. She watched closely and they rounded the far corner, then turned the opposite way and went on.

She looked up at Seth who had his right index finger up to his lips as if to tell everyone to not speak a word. They slowly left Hannah in her designated spot and moved into their appointed hiding positions covering a block radius. Not a sound was heard. According to her calculations, it was a little before 1:00 a.m. Over an hour till time for the mission to strike. She was positioned near an alley in an abandoned store at the corner of Damrak and Amsted. She was shivering, but she wasn't sure if it was the falling temperature or suspense from this crazy mission. Nevertheless, she quietly shivered and dare not move, less she be discovered and blow the whole operation.

Silence. It seemed to be her only comfort. No noise was better than the dreaded sound of soldiers' boots approaching. She silently prayed to God that if He even cared and was listening to her, to please help them survive this and make it a successful mission. Surely, God wanted them to strike at these soldiers who were persecuting His children? The silence continued. More silence. If she hadn't been so nervous and excited, she would have probably fallen asleep. But she sat there continuing to bite frantically on her fingernails.

Finally, she glanced at her watch and realized it was 2:00 a.m. Fifteen minutes till go time. She crouched impatiently in the darkness and peered out of a side window, waiting for the soldiers' shift change and the small window of opportunity for the Resistance to destroy the supply wagon. Within a few minutes, she saw Seth running in the shadows toward the wagon holding what looked like a makeshift homemade bomb. Before she even knew what was really happening, he released the bomb into the side of the wagon and ran like the wind off to the side. Her heart stopped. She held her breath. A few seconds later, an explosion caused chaos to ensue. The soldiers on duty all sprang to action.

Hannah watched as at least a dozen soldiers raced to try and save the supplies in the fiery wagon, but their efforts would be in vain. Her glance darted both ways and then, as planned, while the soldiers were distracted, she ran out the back of the store she was hiding in and raced behind a few Resistance teen members as fast as she could to the meeting point in Damrak Park by a hidden designated bench. They all showed up at the same time and raced into the back woods to make their way backward to the bookshop while the diversion surrounding the explosion sight unfolded.

"Wow, what a rush!" Hannah was in an elated state of shock as the adrenaline pumped her blood through her veins much faster than she expected. She felt so accomplished. The Resistance had accomplished their mission with her help. She didn't really have to do much, but she stayed on guard and did her part. She was ecstatic. Once the group had dispersed quietly and she and Seth were safely in the hidden room with the Dressler's, she couldn't stop smiling or shaking. She gently set the flashlight down on an end table near the bottom of the stairs.

Seth caught his breath and then quietly exclaimed, "Mom, you should have seen it. To see their precious supplies go up in flames was awesome! I was so proud to be a part of the regime. How do you feel, Katie? You were so brave. I'm really quite impressed with you."

Hannah looked at Seth and blushed from the compliment. She grinned from ear to ear. "It was amazing! I feel I could conquer the world!"

Bursting their bubble of triumph, Mr. Dressler gently chided the two teens. "Well, you both put yourselves in grave danger tonight. I know you had your fun, but remember who you are and what role we ultimately must play here. If there was ever any doubt Jews were hidden in Amsterdam, there won't be any more doubts after tonight. Time is of the essence, and we are in even more danger than before. They are going to be very angry now."

"So what? Let them be angry! We are sick of hiding and sick of their existence here. I hope we scared them and they run off like dogs with their tails between their legs!" Seth proclaimed.

"Not likely, son. They are going to want revenge."

"Well, they can bring it on. We will keep coming and hit them where it hurts the most," Seth challenged.

Mr. Dressler warned, "How many lives will be lost in the process? We have to remember it isn't just about us." He looked around the room at the others who were sleeping soundly on their cots.

Hannah wondered herself if it was all for nothing. She questioned to herself, *What did they prove with this strike anyway? Would the Germans really be affected by the loss of their supplies?* She knew she had more to accomplish if she was going to help her new friends. She wasn't sure what was next for the team of Resistance members. The prospect both excited and frightened her. She looked at Seth and he too seemed lost in his own thoughts as the frame of his perfect face was grim in the candlelight.

What would the coming days hold for her? She knew she wasn't athletic like Charlie or smart like Beth. What could she contribute? How could she make a difference for this cause? Then it came to her … Seth had said she was brave. Maybe she could be brave. Maybe that's what she already was—brave. Hannah lay down, smiled to herself, and almost immediately fell into an exhausted sleep.

CHAPTER 6

Adjustments

Hannah awoke that next morning with a terrible headache. It was throbbing so bad she felt dizzy. She told Adelaide about it and immediately, Mrs. Dressler gave her two cups of water to sip on.

"You must be dehydrated, dear," Mrs. Dressler informed her.

Oh, I guess so. I am not used to going this long without water, Hannah thought. "Thank you," was all she replied. After almost an hour, she began to feel better and sat up for prayer and breakfast, which consisted of thick oatmeal that hung in her throat and almost made her gag. She realized that day, more than ever, how much she wanted to go home. Her mom was the best cook and if she were home now, she could imagine having a full breakfast of scrambled eggs, bacon, and French toast. The thought almost made her cry. *Maybe I am not so brave after all,* she thought miserably.

Just then, before she could really wallow in self-pity, Gretchen interrupted her thoughts. "I hear you were wonderful last night. Seth told Papa all about it and I overheard part of it while I was laying down, before everyone else woke up. Seth left already, but said he will try and be back tonight."

"It is risky for him to come here so much," Mrs. Dressler concluded. "I wish he would consider the risks before coming here so often lately."

Adelaide responded thoughtfully, "I like that he comes so much lately. It helps the hiding seem not so bad, Mama."

Mrs. Dressler thought a moment and smiled without speaking. Mrs. Kern was now awake and her children looking up at her expectantly, no doubt wanting some of the dry thick oatmeal. Hannah couldn't understand why, other than severe starvation. The oatmeal had no flavor or taste in her opinion. "Oh well, food is food when you are hungry," she thought sadly.

Since it was still dark outside in the early morning hours, Adelaide begged her mama and papa to let Hannah go with her up to the bookshop to look for some new books to read. They finally agreed after much consideration, and warned the girls to be absolutely quiet and to never go near the large, mostly barred-up windows at the front of the store. They would be allowed only a few minutes up there for fear of a soldier discovering them. The soldiers would be on even more high alert now since the explosion of their supplies.

The girls were thrilled and crept quietly up the creaky stairs to the inner room that opened up by trapdoor and out into the bookshop. Hannah held her breath as she squinted, adjusting her eyes to a different room. Her hands shaking, she followed Adelaide into the bookshop and in the darkness, she tried to see book titles. It was extremely difficult to see, however, a street lamp gave a dim light's shadow so she was able to see some book titles. She browsed around the shop, not making a sound. Adelaide did the same.

Hannah finally chose two books to read. She couldn't make out the whole titles, but the pictures she saw intrigued her. She waited patiently for Adelaide to choose and then the two girls tiptoed out of the bookshop in the back by way of the inner room. She paused long enough to look around and try to figure out how she came to enter this place through this room only a few days before. They headed through the trapdoor, down the creaky stairs, and safely into the hiding room/basement.

The girls spent the morning reading their book choices. Hannah read some of one of her books to Gretchen and Liesel while three of the Kern children also listened shyly to Hannah read the story of a small boy and his adventures on a small farm in Sweden. Milking goats and hay rides in the summer afternoon captivated the children's interest for the morning and before they knew it, they were all hungry for lunch.

Mrs. Dressler said there was only bread and a little oatmeal left for lunch. That did *not* sound appealing to Hannah. She wondered if she could sneak out and steal some fruit or vegetables for them. She knew she saw a small garden back by the park while she was running away from the chaos last night. It was in a very public location and probably used by the Nazis, but she wondered if she dared sneak a few items of produce for her and her new friends. The thought left her, however, when Mr. Dressler came in with a stern look on his face. He pulled Mrs. Dressler over to the side and privately whispered in her ear. Mrs. Kern sat up straight and an even more stern than normal look was on her face. Mr. Kern was not there.

A few minutes later, as the children were finishing their bread and oatmeal, Mr. Dressler left the room. Mrs. Dressler and Mrs. Kern spoke privately and asked to speak to Adelaide and Hannah out of the small children's earshot. "It is good news," Mrs. Dressler assured them. Hannah let out a loud sigh. "The Dressler family have relatives in Sweden who are willing to take them in if we can find a way to smuggle them to the ships leaving the Netherlands for Denmark. Once they reach Denmark, there are people who can smuggle them through Denmark to Sweden by boat."

"Isn't Denmark under military occupation?" Hannah inquired.

"Not yet," Mrs. Dressler confirmed.

Adelaide spoke up, "Hannah, aren't you from Denmark? Were soldiers there when you left?"

Hannah hesitated slightly and turned to her friend, "I haven't been there in years," she lied. "I'm not sure what is going on over there anymore. I know it must be dangerous." She hated to lie, but now was definitely not the time to be honest about where she really was from.

Mrs. Kern spoke up, "More dangerous than it is hiding here in this God-forsaken hole? I don't know a lot about how life is out there right now, but we should go and make the trip to our relatives in Sweden if at all possible." Tears were pouring from her eyes and her body was shaking.

"It is a long and dangerous journey to make with small children, Alice," Mrs. Dressler addressed Mrs. Kern. She hoped her words would soothe the unstable woman.

Between sobs she managed to say, "Greta, we must go. It is best for our family. We can't stay here and go stir crazy in this hole." She must not have seen the look of hurt and indignation in Mrs. Dressler's eyes. This "hole" was the only home they had for now.

After a moment, she sighed. "Yes, I understand, Alice. God will be with you. The plan is to have you all leave tonight. Seth will take you as far as the northern border. There will be a ship waiting for you all there. The Swedes have sent word that handkerchiefs laced with cocaine can confuse and trick the Nazi's dogs' sense of smell. You will all hide in the lower decks of the ship and make the journey to Denmark. This has been a successful practice over there for years without the Germans catching on."

Hannah thought about Denmark and Sweden. Had it been a few years before 1942, she might have even had the opportunity to meet her own great-grandmother and her grandmother "Uma" on a journey like that. She felt certain, however, that they were safely in the United States by 1942. She felt strange at the prospect though. Her mind also raced with the thought of how she, technically, was in a foreign country while all her family was back in America. Well, her parents weren't even born yet, were they? Oh, this is so confusing. Adelaide brought her back to the present.

"Hannah, Seth may need your help tonight getting the Kerns to the boat. Are you willing to help them?" Mrs. Dressler asked.

Hannah looked at the Kern children and her heart ached. "Of course, I will do whatever needs to be done. These kids deserve a better life. I will help in any way I can to make that a possibility," Hannah spoke bravely.

CHAPTER 7

Midnight Run

That evening, as they all sat down for the last time together to say their evening prayer, there was a distinct cloud of sadness hanging low over the group. How, in such a short time, had these people captured her heart so completely? Hannah wondered in amazement. One of the little Kern girls spoke up then in a sweet little voice, "Kay-tee, I will miss you. You read real good, Kay-tee." Hannah smiled up at her, but couldn't say a word back to her due to a large lump stuck in her throat.

They all ate silently. It was a meal of hard cheese, stale crackers, and a special fruit that looked like fig plums or dates. They were dry, but Hannah was happy for another kind of food than the same old bread. Adelaide had mentioned earlier that evening that the Sabbath was tomorrow. She said none of them would be going about after sunrise tomorrow till sunrise the following day, so it was essential that their mission be successful tonight in delivering the Kerns to a boat, and be back safely before sunrise. Hannah had learned also that day that the Kerns had not been in hiding with the Dressler family long. A year at the most. They came from another hideout. Apparently, there were Jews hiding in places all over the city of Amsterdam. Hannah had felt foolish and naïve when she came to this realization. How else were the rest of the members of the Resistance never caught? Of course, there were scattered hiding spots throughout the city. She should have known that.

Actually, as they ate together, toward the end of their meal, Mr. Dressler mentioned that a small group of Jews were found just that very afternoon hiding in an attic of a store a few blocks away. They had been shipped immediately to the ghetto awaiting the next train to a concentration camp. Mrs. Dressler began to cry softly. Mrs. Kern looked like she had seen a ghost. Hannah wondered if the Jews caught were any members of the Resistance.

As if to answer her unasked question, Mr. Kern spoke up, "It was an elderly couple. They had no children with them. It was just as well in some respects. They were starving with large rats, the size of a small cat or dog, up there in the attic eating all their scraps of food."

Hannah shuttered, "Large rats? Eww!" She thought she was about to be sick. She almost lost her meal altogether. She quickly pulled herself from the theory of relieving her meal and turned to the eldest Kern child on her left. He was probably seven or eight years old. He had almost sandy brown hair with clear, hazel eyes. She realized she had not seen him smile the whole time she had known him. She so desperately wanted to see him smile. His eyes looked haunted.

Hannah confided in him then, "Do you know what the sky looks like over the water? The stars are so clear that they reflect like speckles of light glimmering over the big ocean of glass. You will be able to see hundreds of stars at night on the water. Can I tell you a secret? I envy you. Truly, I do. I wish I could go with you on your upcoming journey. You must write to me when you reach Sweden and tell me all about it."

The little boy's eyes glowed with excitement and fascination. Hannah looked to Adelaide across the table and she smiled sincerely at Hannah. Hannah smiled back and slightly shrugged her shoulders. She tried to keep the atmosphere as carefree as possible, considering the circumstances.

After dinner, they all watched the Kern family pack their little bag of belongings. Then, they all sat around and Mr. Dressler opened up his Bible. He read from the book of Psalm. He read aloud so eloquently, "I will instruct you and teach you in the way you should go; I will counsel you and watch over you, Psalm 32:8."

Mr. Kern spoke up then, "I believe the Lord will be with us. The God of Abraham, Isaac, and Jacob goes before us and will get us safely to Sweden. There is no need to fear. He goes before us and stands beside us."

No one said a word. Hannah felt a sense of peace she never had experienced before. She somehow knew God was in control and as dangerous as their mission was going to be, He would guide them as He promised to guide David. They all laid down to rest for it was going to be a busy night. After a few hours of sleep, Hannah was woken up by Seth, who gently nudged her shoulder. "Katie, it's time." She looked up and saw the Kerns all standing ready to leave and their family, Mr. Dressler, Mrs. Dressler, Adelaide, and Seth all stood hugging each other goodbye. Hannah stood slowly and reached out to hug Adelaide. "I will see you in the morning," Hannah spoke softly.

Adelaide replied, "Do be so very careful, Hannah, I mean, dear Katie. See you before sunrise." They hugged again.

She had a thought and asked Adelaide, "What is your non-Jewish alias? Mine is Katie, but I don't even know yours."

"Kristina," Adelaide replied with a slight smile.

Hannah turned and quickly hugged Mrs. Dressler. The two younger Dressler girls were sleeping. They didn't want to wake them. The Kern family, Seth, and Hannah quietly left the room by ascending the stairs and making their way out of hiding. Instead of turning to the bookshop door, they turned to the right and went through another door to the back of the shop. Hannah waited patiently for Seth to peer out cautiously. He had said there would be Resistance members stationed in random spots to help them make the transition to the woods and through them to the several miles journey that would lead them to the sea, where the boat was docked to take the Kern family to Denmark.

Once the coast was clear, for Seth received the "all clear" signal from a Resistance member, they all ventured out without a sound onto the Amsterdam alleyway street that ran behind the bookshop. Their trip to the woods was quiet and they slipped along, without difficulty, in the shadows. She thought, *The soldiers must not be as alert as normal due to tomorrow being the Sabbath. They must think any Jews nearby will be inactive during this time.* Hannah reasoned to herself that she must not let her guard down, however quiet the streets seemed to be.

Once they were all safely in the woods, they could all breathe a little easier, but still they were to make no sound at all. Hannah almost tripped a few times over the tree roots in their path. A few times the children seemed to almost be about to whine, but Hannah, who lead up the rear of their little group, would grab their hands and put her finger to her lips to signal them to be quiet. They all seemed to obey and treaded on into the night.

After what seemed like hours and hours, but in reality, was only maybe forty-five minutes to an hour tops, they noticed the trees and terrain changing. The ground began to be softer and another mile or two, and they could hear waves crashing the shore just ahead. Once they stopped at the edge of the woods, Seth told them in a hushed whisper that there would be soldiers near the boats. He removed a backpack from his shoulder. Hannah had not realized till just now that he had been carrying it on his back. He had a cart also that was off to one side, concealed by thick tree branches.

They each gave quick exchange of hugs and then Seth and Hannah helped each Kern family member climb into the cart and he gave them several white handkerchiefs to hold. He then put a large tarp over them and used buckets with fishing net and gear to place gently on top of the tarp to make the soldiers believe he was bringing the gear to the fishermen. The children shifted slightly and Hannah patted their backs. She whispered, "It will all be okay. The Lord goes before you. Remember, don't forget to write when you make it safely to Sweden." She said this, knowing full well, she would never receive a letter. Even if they made it safely to Sweden. They didn't even really know who she was, much less her mailing address in New Hampshire.

Seth drew out a blond hair piece, like a wig of short blond hair. He placed it securely on his head, then turned to Hannah. "Does it look all right, Katie? Do I pass for a native Netherland boy taking gear to local fishermen?"

Hannah reached up and adjusted the wig slightly. "Yes. Definitely believable," she said smiling.

He stared back at her and for a brief moment, she thought he might kiss her. He moved to the right and grabbed the wagon by its handles. He turned slightly back to her then. "Wait right here for me and don't make a sound. If you think for a moment someone is coming this way, or if something goes wrong and you hear commotion, turn and run back as fast as you can. I left little white pieces of cloth on our way by the trail. Follow it and you will find your way back to Amsterdam, if something should happen to me."

Hannah felt like she might faint at the thought. Instead, she smiled at him and watched him ease the wagon toward the beach and smoothly descend to the boat ramp. German soldiers were posted checking everything by cart and wagon with their dogs sniffing frantically. The handkerchiefs must have been laced with cocaine to deter the dogs' smell because they sniffed a second or two at the wagon the Kerns were inside of and went on. Seth calmly pushed it to a designated boat. The ship captain helped him lift the heavy wagon onto his boat. Hannah breathed a sigh of relief. She hadn't realized she was holding her breathe that entire time he took them down to the boat. Once Seth spoke casually to a few of the crew, he turned to venture back to the woods.

A soldier stopped him halfway back. Hannah felt panic rise in her throat. Seth couldn't be captured! She remembered the scripture about the Lord being with them. She silently lifted a request to God. "Please, God, let us make it safely back to the bookshop together. I'm scared and not sure what to do. We need Your help. Also, please let the Kern family make it safely to Sweden. Amen."

Just then, Seth turned and passed a few other soldiers who spoke casually to him, thinking all the while he was a Netherland boy. Just before he reached the safe edge of the woods, a dog barked toward where she stood from the shore. Hannah froze. The soldier holding the dog approached Seth. "Hail Hitler!" he called out and made a strange hand gesture in the air above his head. Seth repeated the phrase and motion without hesitation.

The soldier asked if Seth was alone and he said, "Yes. I am heading back to my father's pig farm a mile away." The soldier looked Seth square in the face and looked toward the woods where Hannah was concealed in the thick brush.

Should she run, or should she stay and wait for Seth? Her hands became clammy and she thought she may faint. The soldier hesitated again and then, after a moment, finally said, "Well, run along, boy, and help your father tend the pigs. We may come looking for a good meal sometime soon, and you can feed us a swine or two." He scoffed a laugh with a sadistic tone.

Hannah shivered slightly as Seth laughed and responded, "Aye, sir. Will do. Come anytime." Then he turned and walked into the thick wood.

They traveled quietly back to Amsterdam through the woods. Hannah noticed Seth reached out for her arm every now and then to help her keep her balance on the rough path of rocks and tree branches. She caught him looking at her several times, but she had to keep her focus on reaching the end of the wooded path. He was so handsome and so brave, not like the boys she went to school with back home. He was so determined to help the cause of the Jews and save his family. She thought he was so noble and true to his convictions. When they were able to be in a spot where they could speak in a whisper, she asked him if he thought they would return before the sun came up. She remembered this was the Sabbath, and they needed to be back safely before the sunrise.

Seth said he felt they would be back by then. He asked her a few questions she had difficulty answering honestly. He asked about her family and her life. She told him she had a dad, mom, one older sister, and a younger brother. She kept her guard up as to not give away her true identity. He said she had a most interesting accent. This made her nervous because she felt self-conscious that she sounded too much like an American. However, she soon realized he had never met an American, so he wouldn't know what an American sounded like anyway.

She wanted to keep the conversation going, so she asked him if he had ever seen a castle. He said he had, but he had never been inside one. She told him she would love to see a castle and tour inside one someday. He told her tours of castles were forbidden during war time, but when the war ended, they could go inside one sometime. She couldn't explain why, but that made her heart happy.

Just then, as they were edging from the woods, she saw the slightest bit of sun and colors of the sunrise just entering the eastern horizon. She looked at the sun awakening as if mesmerized by its beauty. She smiled and closed her eyes. She felt God's presence for the first time in her life. She wanted to sit down and watch the sun make its grand entrance all the way into the eastern sky, but Seth gently nudged her on to the street. They cautiously edged their way among the shadows and she could see the door that opened into the back of the bookshop in the alleyway. They reached it, and just as she walked into it with Seth on her heels, he turned her around inside the little room. He looked at her expectantly for a second and then softly kissed her lips. He then turned and left her standing in the room alone as he made his way out the same door they came in from the alley. She couldn't move or even breathe. She was paralyzed in complete shock. After gaining her bearings, she eased herself through the trapdoor and gently down the flight of stairs into the hidden room. Her legs were shaking, and she felt that she might fall flat on her face at any moment. Mr. and Mrs. Dressler and the children were waiting for her at the bottom of the stairs. The children had just awoken, and they were all praying for their safe return. When Hannah entered, they all lit up with delight and begin to question her.

"Where's Seth?" Mr. Dressler asked anxiously.

"He just saw me to the door and left. He is safe. I assume we will see him again soon," Hannah answered with a smile on her lips.

"Wonderful! Come sit, darling. You must be famished. It is the Sabbath Day, so we have a surprise breakfast for you, dear." Mrs. Dressler directed her to sit down before a magnificent feast of biscuits and fruit jelly.

CHAPTER 8

Negotiations

Sabbath Day came and went quietly. Hannah and the Dressler family spent a lot of time praying and talking among each other. It was a pleasant, relaxing day other than the fact that Seth never came at all that evening. They all had expected him to show up, and when the day came and went and it was the next morning, there was slight concern for his well-being. Mrs. Dressler explained to Hannah that before she came, they were used to going days and even sometimes weeks without seeing Seth, and they learned to trust God to intervene and take care of their oldest child.

They had all become used to his presence, and when he never showed and three days had come and gone, it was clear something could be wrong. The evening of the third day, Mr. Dressler spoke to Mrs. Dressler in hushed tones about sending an inquiry after Seth's whereabouts the very next day. Just as they were getting ready for bed, the door at the top of the stairs creaked open and Seth, followed by a family of three people no one knew, came down the stairs slowly and entered the hidden room.

Seth began to explain, "Dad, this is Mr. and Mrs. Engelberg and their daughter, Amelia. They are Jews who are traveling through the area on their way to the coast. Like the Kerns, they plan to stay a while and then book passage to Denmark on their way to Sweden. I figured we could accommodate them here for a short time till we can help them make arrangements for passage to Denmark."

Mrs. Dressler grabbed Seth and hugged him tight. No words were exchanged, only hugs. When he got to Hannah, he stopped slightly, grinned like a schoolboy, and hugged her. Adelaide noticed it right off that there was a difference in the way the two teens interacted. She tucked that knowledge away for inquisitive questions for Hannah later.

This new family seemed sweet and much more social than the Kerns. They all got along well together. After they had been there for a few days, Mr. Dressler began to meet secretly with a few connections he had in the shipping business to get a passage for the Engelberg family to Denmark. He learned it would be a few more weeks before another ship was available to take Jews as hidden passage across the sea. The fishermen and ship captains were smart in only allowing a certain number of people and ships to be transporting at a time. Their goal was to smuggle just enough to rescue but throw off any suspicion the Nazis might have.

Seth came as often as he could. He tried not to be too obvious in his growing affections for Hannah. Something inside him, however, kept him coming more regularly for visits, regardless of the increasing dangers. He was working effortlessly with the Resistance to establish another covert operation to blow up the train tracks before the next incoming train carrying German supplies and cargo was to arrive in a week away. A part of him wanted to recruit Hannah, but he knew how dangerous this was going to be, and the likelihood of getting caught was growing by the day. He would not risk her life again and put her in any more danger. Even though she didn't seem to be who she said she was, he feared for her life more than his own.

Hannah saw Seth's distance as a sign that he wasn't as interested in her as she was in him. What was she doing here? Would she be here forever? There were days when she became so homesick for her family she almost couldn't breathe. She worried her family was sick from fright for her safety, but just refused to let her mind go there for any length of time or she would go stir crazy.

One day, while the girls were in the bookshop browsing through the fictions novels, Adelaide asked Hannah about Seth. "You guys seemed to be close the other day when he hugged you."

Hannah's cheeks turned pink, and she whispered back to her friend, "He is a good friend. I thought it could be more for him, but I realize friendship is what we both want right now."

Adelaide paused before responding, "Hmm. He definitely likes you, Hannah. I can see it in his eyes when he is in a room with you."

Hannah smiled but dismissed the idea quickly. She would be going home soon. She could feel it. She knew she couldn't make sense of anything other than friendship with Seth when she knew they could never be together. She was from a whole other world. A different time and place. She needed to focus on helping in any way she could, and get back home soon. Home seemed to be almost a memory now. She needed to focus on going home soon. Her real family needed her.

The girls went quietly back down the stairs to the hidden room and helped Mrs. Dressler get the younger girls ready for bed. Hannah wondered when the next covert mission would be. She knew the time was soon that the railroad tracks would need to be blown up. But when? She hoped Seth included her in the plans. If she wasn't able to help, then what was the point in her being there in the first place?

After everyone had gone to bed, she lay awake wondering about everything in the darkness. Only a small candle was lit tonight. After a while of restless wondering, she heard a soft sound at the door above the stairs. She saw Seth climbing quietly down and spoke softly to Mr. Dressler, who Hannah thought had been asleep.

"I realize that, Dad, but how do I avoid it? We need her help. We may not pull this off without her," Seth argued.

Mr. Dressler warned, "Son, you realize you all may be caught this time. You could be killed immediately. They shoot traitors in the back of the head in the middle of the streets. You know the risks. I do not want to see any of my children, any children for that matter, be killed. It isn't worth it, son."

"I know, Dad, but we have to do this. I need Hannah and Adelaide this time. Please, Dad. If we don't do this, we may all be captured anyway. She can handle it, I just … I know it. Trust me."

After several minutes, she heard Mr. Dressler reply, "Okay, Seth. I will speak with them first thing in the morning. Come by tomorrow evening to see us before bedtime if possible, to cover final details with them. When is it supposed to happen?"

"Two days' time at eighteen hundred hours," Seth explained.

"Okay, son. Please be careful and take care of yourself. You look too skinny. Are you eating?"

"When I can, I eat. I am more worried about you all." He glanced at Hannah and saw her eyes open, watching them. He smiled at her and his smile melted her from within. She smiled back as he turned to leave. That kiss did mean something to him. She knew that now.

The next day, Mr. Dressler took Adelaide and Hannah up to the secret room above the stairs to speak privately with them. He explained that the Resistance planned to blow up the tracks to the Amsterdam train station about three miles outside of town in two days' time. He told them both that Seth needed their help. Hannah was surprised to see how excited Adelaide was at the prospect of being involved in the Resistance mission.

"You both know the risks," Mr. Dressler stated flatly. "I see no other choice, but I'll be honest. I don't like the idea of either of you girls being involved. You could be captured. You could lose your lives. Do you both understand? Adelaide, I don't want you telling your mother about your involvement right now. She would have a fit. For now, let's keep it between us."

Both girls agreed and were told to wait for Seth to come visit that night to give them more details about the operation. As they waited, Hannah realized the full depth of the danger that lay ahead. She resolved to give everything to the Lord. She prayed a silent prayer to God that evening, asking Him to come into her life and save her.

Hannah's Prayer

"Lord, take control and be my God. I am tired of fighting You and I know how much I need You to forgive me and be my Savior. I love you, Lord. No matter what happens from now on, my life is in Your hands. Amen." Her tears of joy flowed freely.

CHAPTER 9

The Resistance Strikes Again

The two days flew by, and before Hannah knew it, she and Adelaide were preparing to meet up with the other members of the Resistance to take action against the Germans by blowing up their train tracks just a few miles from the Amsterdam train station on the edge of town. Hannah was more nervous than normal but kept her mood light and confident for Adelaide. This was Adelaide's first covert operation, and she was beyond thrilled to help. Mrs. Dressler was not as thrilled.

"How could you be okay with this?" Mrs. Dressler asked Mr. Dressler anxiously. Tears were in her eyes. "She is our daughter. You said once that you would never allow her to be in the Resistance."

To which he responded, "Greta, they need both the girls. Several Resistance members have been captured or fallen ill. They need the numbers. All of our safety is in jeopardy. The supplies coming on the train will be used to make bombs against us. You know that it needs to be destroyed." The subject was finally dropped then.

Hannah and Adelaide read early bedtime stories to Gretchen and Liesel before leaving at sundown. They kissed each girl and crept quietly up the stairs to the room behind the bookshop that led out to the back alleyway. Mrs. Dressler cried silent tears and held on to Adelaide for what seemed like eternity. Mr. Dressler cautiously warned the girls to stay in the alley until they saw Seth, who was due to come get them there shortly. The girls obeyed and waited quietly in the alley for what seemed like ages.

Finally, Seth inched his way toward the alley. His own heart was racing, but he knew this mission was necessary. He wondered if it was the mission or the thought of seeing Hannah, umm Katie, that made his heart truly race. When he reached the girls waiting for him, they all smiled briefly at each other and proceeded to the route they were to take in the dark shadows to where they were to rendezvous with the other Resistance members to carry out this dangerous task.

They all were in place and were all given assignments. This would take the work of every member to be successful. Hannah looked to Adelaide to see how she was adjusting to this new environment. She smiled at her friend, and Adelaide smiled confidently back. This was a mission that could very well kill them all should they be caught; however, they all knew it was possible to make a huge handicap in the Nazi troops occupation should their mission be a success. The two girls were given black jackets to wear over their clothing. The jackets were rough and smelled of must and tobacco. They didn't seem to mind though. They were far too excited and nervous to pay much attention to the jackets other than to know it would help them go undetected in the darkness.

Twenty minutes had gone by. Hannah's job was to help Seth and another guy she didn't know place the bombs strategically along the tracks. It seemed easy enough, but Seth stressed to her that it was very dangerous because the bombs were ready to blow within seconds once they were ignited with a match. She followed the guys' lead and placed the five bombs she was responsible for along the left side of the train tracks. Once the fifteen bombs were all in place, a few inches apart up and down the tracks on both left and right sides, they would all move to the edge of the woods about a hundred yards away and wait for the sound of the train approaching. They would hear the train, followed by a whistle, and that would signal the four older members—Seth, a brown-headed girl Annalise she recognized from the other mission they worked together a few weeks before, and two boys she wasn't familiar with—to race to the bombs, light a match to ignite the bombs, and run like a marathon sprint in the opposite direction of Hannah and Adelaide as they all run away from the tracks as quickly as possible. Hannah and Adelaide were to wait for the bombs to be ignited and then run as fast as they could toward the city and don't stop till they reached the bookshop. Seth would come by as soon as it was safe and check on them later that night.

The plan was going smoothly with the bombs in place. Suddenly, they all heard the grind of train wheels to metal iron track chugging at a steady but quick pace. The members carrying unlit matches began to run full speed toward the tracks. Three of the members successfully lit their matches, but Seth couldn't get one of his matches to ignite the five bombs on his side. Frantically, he fumbled for another match. The girl who had lit hers, acting quickly, jumped to Seth's side and light his bombs. The other members of the Resistance had run off, as Hannah and Adelaide should have, but the girls stood paralyzed as the train whistle blew shrilly in the night air to signal its fast approach. Hannah couldn't take her eyes off Seth. Adelaide stood frozen in fear by her side. Neither girl could move.

Once all the bombs minus one dud was lit, Seth and the girl ran off in the opposite direction of the girls. Seth must have assumed they had already left. In a split second, Hannah was being dragged by Adelaide in the opposite direction, running as fast as they could. The train whistle was deafening when …

Boom! Boom!

Explosions filled the night. Fire blazed as the iron metal of the tracks were dissipated into the thick smoke. The force of the explosion threw the girls into the air and further into the woods. Hannah hit the ground on her back in a grassy spot in the woods. She looked frantically for Adelaide. She saw her lying facedown on the ground. She wasn't moving. Hannah had a trickle of blood on her hand and a ringing in her ears, but ignored it and rushed to Adelaide's side. She nudged her, urging her friend to wake up. "Adelaide, we have to hurry. The soldiers will be coming for us. Wake up! Hurry!"

Suddenly, Seth was by her side. "What happened?" Seth asked in a panic, looking at his sister and then Hannah's bloody hand.

Hannah couldn't answer other than tears streaming down her face. Suddenly, Adelaide opened her eyes and rolled over. Seth helped her up and urged her to try to stand. Hannah helped him to lift Adelaide, but she couldn't stand. It appeared her ankle had twisted when she fell and was possibly broken.

"We have to hurry!" Hannah demanded.

Seth lifted his sister up over his shoulder and they quickly ran as fast as they could back down the path to the city. They kept within the shadows of the woods and were forced to stop twice to give Seth and Adelaide several breaks. In what seemed like miles, they finally arrived at the edge of the wood, just beyond the streets that would take them to the alleyway. As they approached the streets to step out of the woods, they quickly noticed a soldier stationed at the corner of the alley behind the bookshop.

"What do we do?" Hannah asked Seth in a quiet, distressed tone.

Just before Seth could respond, a young man who they recognized as one of the Resistance members, snuck up behind the soldier and before they knew what was happening, he shot the soldier in the head.

Hannah flinched and hid her face behind Seth. She recovered quickly and they looked in every direction before stepping out of the wood, and cautiously edged toward the alley. The Resistance member dragged the soldier over to the door of the back of the bookshop in an effort to hide the body. It began to pour down rain. They all made it safely inside the back of the bookshop, though they were all drenched. Seth carried Adelaide down to the basement where they had their hidden home. He and the Resistance member, who Hannah learned a while later was named Peter, grabbed a towel and some water, and ran back upstairs as Hannah descended. She wasn't sure what the boys were going to do with the soldier's corpse, but her top concern was Adelaide. She checked on her friend, who now sat up with her ankle propped up by pillows. Mrs. Dressler was attending to her daughter and Mr. Dressler made his way up the stairs to help the boys with the mess there.

Adelaide went on and on to her mother about how wonderful it was to be a part of the mission and how she thought they were all surely dead when the bombs exploded. Mrs. Dressler handed

Hannah a wet cloth to wipe her face and clean up. After gaining her composure, Hannah ventured upstairs to the lavoratory at the back of the bookshop to properly clean up. She striped off the black jacket and used the wet washcloth to clean herself and with hands shaking, she then used a comb to brush the twigs and dirt from her hair.

A short time later, she made her way back down the stairs to her cot. She noticed there was no sign of the boys or Mr. Dressler. She saw Adelaide asleep sitting up. She looked around and realized everyone but Mrs. Dressler were asleep. The Engelberg family were all slightly snoring in their sleep. She found her cot and yawned. Mrs. Dressler told Hannah she should sleep because it was close to dawn now. As she began to lay down, Mr. Dressler and Seth descended into the room.

Hannah sat back up and stared anxiously at them. Seth came to sit beside her and held her hand. No words were spoken between the two of them, but Hannah was slightly embarrassed that he made such a show of affection in front of his parents. They didn't seem to mind or notice the two teenagers. Seth glanced at Hannah's other hand that had a deep cut on it from the explosion. She had attempted to clean it up earlier in the lavoratory. He looked into her eyes and her smile assured him she was fine.

Mr. Dressler mentioned that they burned the body of the soldier in a secluded area of the woods, but they figured the fire would soon be discovered by the other Nazis. There would, no doubt, be retaliation from the German soldiers now over the death of their brother-in-arms. The question remained as to whether the soldiers were on to them or thought it was a random act. Only time would tell.

CHAPTER 10

Retaliation

The next day, word reached them through a private connection that Mr. Dressler had, that the Germans' supply train, as well as a large portion of the train tracks, was destroyed in the bombing. So far, the discovery of the dead German soldier remained a mystery. It was rumored that the Russian leader, Stalin, and the German leader, Hitler, were at an impasse on negotiations in the war. Some Germans believed the Russians were behind the attacks the Resistance were carrying out.

This was great news for the Resistance. It meant the Germans weren't on to them as of now. Hitler's bullying and growing paranoia made the Russians seem to be the likely enemy. Hitler had made a great many enemies in his conquest to claim world domination and the alienation of the Jews. His hatred for them was so inhumane, that most people thought it was impossible for one man to be so evil and on such a personal mission to destroy an entire race.

Hannah was simply baffled at how wrong she herself had been about Hitler. She thought while she read history books and studied Hitler, that the books must have been written for drama or by someone who had a personal dislike of the man, but in reality, she saw everything in a very different light. How could she tell everyone back home of her new experiences? Would she even make it back home? Would she survive, and if she did, would she somehow be stuck over here? She loved the Dressler family, but she ached for her own family and her home. How could she be in two places and times at once? It was so confusing for her. She knew she was there to help these kind people, but she did not understand. "Why me?" she often wondered.

The next day, the sounds of bomber planes overhead and then bombs exploding, rattled the building. Everyone in the hidden room was terrified. This was clearly an invasion. Were they being bombed by the Russians, German, British soldiers? No one knew to be exact at that moment. Another explosion echoed off the walls and the two youngest Dressler girls began to cry softly and Amelia, the Engelbergs' young daughter, cried as well. Mr. Dressler came running down the stairs with Mr. Engelberg at his heels.

"We are being invaded! Everyone get down!" Mr. Engelberg ordered.

"Seth! Where is Seth?" Mrs. Dressler cried out to her husband.

Hannah became even more panicked and cried to herself and to God in distress. "Seth! Lord, please keep him safe." Hannah recognized the look of fear in Adelaide's eyes.

"Who is bombing us?" Mrs. Engelberg asked her husband in terror.

"We aren't sure, dear," he replied patiently.

Finally, the bombing subsided. The candles had been knocked over and the lamps blown out. It was completely dark in their hidden room, but Hannah knew they were alive because she could feel her pulse rapidly beating and hear the breathing of the others all huddled together with her in a corner. She wondered how long they all sat there shaking and waiting for another explosion. When none came, Mrs. Dressler lit a candle and a lamp that had been knocked over and the glass cover was broken. Everyone squinted and looked about slowly. Books were everywhere and Hannah could only imagine what the bookshop looked like upstairs. They all gained their bearings and began to move about carefully.

It was several hours later when Mr. Dressler assumed it was dark outside, that he ventured up the stairs to assess the bookshop. "Can Hannah and I come also, Papa? Please," Adelaide begged her father. He agreed and the three of them plus Mr. Engelberg all dreadfully ventured up the stairs. When Hannah stepped into the bookshop, her heart sank. All the beautiful books were thrown about the room in a haphazard fashion due to the explosions all around the city. She looked to Adelaide, who was staring out the window past the curtains at all the destruction about the city. The church down the street was destroyed with the steeple laying on the road in a heap of brick rubble. She saw a tear escape and make its way down Adelaide's cheek.

The group assessed the damage as best they could and then quietly ventured back down the stairs. *What a devastating loss*, Hannah thought, *all those wonderful books were missing pages, ruined from being thrown about and bent helter-skelter.* She felt such sadness in her heart for the Dressler family that she could barely breathe. Her chest ached with the pain of the loss they all must surely feel.

Later that evening, Mr. Dressler began to try and analyze the attack. Who could have done this? He spoke softly to Mrs. Dressler, "The Germans are the most obvious, if they have been made aware of the Resistance, but I often wonder now if the Russians were not the ones behind it? Also, we must consider the British Army. They have our Dutch Prime Minister, Pieter Gerbrandy, in exile. Could the British soldiers have sent the bombers to destroy us?" Mrs. Dressler was most concerned as well, but her top priority was the safety and whereabouts of her son, Seth.

Knowing full well that it was out of their hands, and the fate of them all hung in the Lord's hands, Mrs. Dressler offered that they all say a special prayer of thanksgiving for their survival through the invasion and for the safety of Seth and all the other Jews scattered throughout. They spent several hours in prayer. Hannah felt that calming peace that could only come from the Lord. She knew Seth had to be out there safe somewhere. He just had to be.

C H A P T E R   1 1

German Headquarters Relocated

The two families hidden in the basement of the bookshop had always been afraid that their hideout would be in jeopardy, but they were not prepared for the day after the bombing. They were woken up early to the sounds of footsteps above them. Harsh clicks of soldiers' boots made everyone sit up anxiously and stare with terror about the room. What were the soldiers doing in the bookshop? Their whole hideout was in grave danger of being discovered. They had not heard from Seth either since before the bombings the day before. The tension in the hidden room was unbearable.

Suddenly, Mr. Dressler crept up the stairs and disappeared into the invisible room just behind the bookshop. Many minutes passed without a word from anyone. Suddenly, they all jumped at the sound of Mr. Dressler descending the stairs. He was alone, thank goodness, and everyone held their breath as they waited patiently for any information he may have overheard. He looked about the room and commanded everyone to come close to him in a circle and he began to whisper. "The Nazis are here. From what I overheard them saying, this is their new command center. The old one was destroyed by a bomb. They are taking up command in the bookshop. They think it is vacant. We will have to see what kind of hours they will keep here. We will have to remain down here and be completely quiet. We are in luck that we have no babies here now. A baby's cry would be the end of us. The secret door leading down here is our only ally, I am afraid

50

to say. We must ration our food and pray Seth stays out of sight as well. We can't risk being caught. It will mean all of our lives ended. Every one of us," he informed us all.

Everyone looked from person to person without a word. Survival took on a whole new meaning for the group that day. Danger was now right upstairs. Silence was of the essence. Not a word, cry, or slight movement that could be heard upstairs was allowed. They all sat down to eat extremely small portions of their food for they knew it would be a while before they would get anything else to eat or drink. The lavoratory that was upstairs would also have to be off limits until the soldiers left for the night. They all prayed that the soldiers would vacate the bookshop all together during the night, or things could really get miserable.

Luckily, as the day came and went and night crept up on them, the soldiers all seemed to be gone. Mr. Dressler and Mr. Engelberg ventured up to check and make sure the coast was clear. They all needed to use the lavoratory and were praying Seth would bring food for them tonight. They were informed by Mr. Dressler that the soldiers were all gone. They quickly all took turns using the lavoratory and ate a late supper of beans or lentils and stale bread. Hannah's throat ached, and she wasn't sure if it was the hard bread, or if she was getting sick. As the night crept on, she felt she may pass out until suddenly, Seth descended the stairs. Hugs were exchanged between the young man and his family. He hugged Hannah last and kissed her cheek. "You made it," Hannah whispered in his ear, gaining her bearings back to her. He smiled.

Seth had been in the woods sleeping when the bombers invaded the day before. He was worried sick and came by twice to scope out the bookshop to make sure it hadn't been damaged by the bombs. Today, he noticed the soldiers and quickly figured out they had taken up command in the building. He feared they would suspect him, even with his Danish wig on, so he kept out of sight in the rubble across the street until the soldiers all abandoned their command. He told them all of the buildings that were destroyed by the bombs. Grocery stores, the library, churches, and the synagogue had major damage from the bombs. Many houses were destroyed and lives lost.

"It's the strangest thing, Dad. I thought the Russians were invading, but from the woods, we were able to see the bomber planes and they weren't Russian. They were German bombers," Seth admitted.

"Germans?" Mr. Engelberg questioned. "Why would they bomb an area they already had control over? Do you think they are on to the Resistance?"

"It is honestly hard to say," Seth replied. "It definitely came as a surprise to everyone. They haven't come into the woods looking for us."

Mrs. Dressler warned, "Not yet, son. They probably will soon though. Maybe you should stay here a few days. Just to be safe."

Seth interjected, "I thought about that myself. I just don't know if the other Resistance members need my help."

"Your safety is of the upmost importance here, son," Mr. Dressler concluded.

It was then decided that Seth would stay several days and nights in the hidden room with them. To risk being caught now when the soldiers were obviously on high alert was simply too risky. Hannah took advantage of the time with him around to read with him and talk about God and their shared interests. They could not visit amongst each other during the day, only at night. Hannah and the others made the habit of sleeping during the day and being up at night to visit and move around. The soldiers occupied the upstairs bookshop from 8:00 a.m. till 5:00 p.m. They rotated shifts for lunch hour, so it was best for the hidden families to sleep during the day.

Except for the occasional nightmare that Amelia Engelberg had, where she had to be soothed from tears and cautioned not to cry out, they all slept somewhat peacefully during those days. This went on like this for several weeks. Seth came and went. Always bringing food back with him. The Engelberg family's escape by sea was postponed for now. It was just too much of a risk and the sea captains were making fewer and fewer smuggling efforts due to the tight Nazi security at the docks.

The days all kind of ran together for Hannah. Adelaide wrote in a journal or doodled sketches as if she was writing a story. The two younger Dressler girls played quietly during the night with makeshift dolls who wore soiled dresses. The Engelberg daughter, Amelia, who couldn't be more than nine or ten years old, colored on the walls. She was quite artistic and used her talents to sketch pictures on the walls and had Gretchen and Liesel try and guess what she was drawing. It passed the time for them and she was grateful to help.

One day, in probably mid-March, the German Nazi soldiers made a racket upstairs, banging and jostling things all around. The sounds of their radio communicators stopped and it was surprising for being mid-day. It woke everyone up that was in hiding down below the bookshop. After a spell, Mr. Dressler ventured upstairs to return with good news. The soldiers had mysteriously and, most suddenly, abandoned the bookshop. What luck! They were gone, at least for now. Everyone quietly celebrated with hope in their hearts.

Finding a Balance

Even with the soldiers gone from the bookshop, the parents felt it best that they all keep sleeping hours during the day and active time continue at night. This was for the sake of their safety and also since the children had become accustomed to this new sleeping pattern. In those nights, Hannah and Adelaide spent much time talking and Hannah learned so much about the restrictions the Jews had been under, even before being forced into hiding. Adelaide freely shared with Hannah how life was before her family lost their freedom.

Adelaide spoke of how it was a slow transition from normal life as a Jew to being dehumanized in Amsterdam. She spoke of how the Germans started the downfall of the Jews inconspicuously by forcing them to get rid of their bicycles. She then spoke of how the Jews were forbidden to use trains, and even ride in cars. She spoke of how her family and any other Jews were required to do their shopping between 3:00 and 5:00 p.m. only, and they were only allowed to go to Jewish-owned barbershops and beauty parlors for their haircuts.

Soon after that, the Jews were forbidden to be out on the streets between 8:00 p.m. and 6:00 a.m. She recalled the time when it became forbidden for them to attend theaters, movies, or any other forms of entertainment. This was especially hard for Adelaide and her family because they loved to visit the local theatre to see plays. Adelaide confided in Hannah that she would love to be an actress in a play. Hannah felt her friend would make a great actress. Her friend was lovely and had a theatrical presence about her. She would dominate the stage, if the opportunity ever presented itself to her.

Next, Hannah learned that the Jews were forbidden to use swimming pools, tennis courts, hockey fields, or any other athletic fields. She learned that Seth was an excellent athlete, before it was forbidden. Adelaide said she used to love to watch her brother compete in athletic competitions. The Dressler family used to go to a local lake on Saturdays, but soon, the Jews were forbidden to go rowing. Jews were forbidden to take part in any athletic activity in public, which included fun activities in the local lakes and parks. One of the hardest things for Mrs. Dressler had been when Jews were forbidden to sit in their gardens or those of their friends after 8:00 p.m. Mrs. Dressler used to love to have garden parties at their home. Hannah learned their home was raided by the Germans shortly after the Dressler's vacated it. Mr. Dressler had left a note there making it seem like he had taken his family and fled the country.

Hannah listened to all the stories and felt pangs of sadness at what her friends had gone through. She also felt anger and resentment at Hitler and his German Nazi soldiers. Her thoughts raced constantly. "Who did they think they were to come invade and take over people's lives like this? What a bully; no worse than a bully—a monster! Pure evil must be driving him to do this to all these innocent people and why? Just because they were Jews? They never did anything to him." Now, more than ever, she knew she was doing the right thing by helping these people. She just wondered about all the other Jews who were being persecuted and didn't have anyone to help them and stand up for them. It drove her to be even more convicted for the Resistance's cause.

As these days passed, Hannah could see how visibly uncomfortable Mrs. Engelberg was becoming with the close-knit quarters of the hidden room below the bookshop. She seemed more irritable than normal and nervous. She said things leading the others to believe she would soon succumb to paranoia, if she continued to think and talk as she did lately. Her husband tried to soothe and comfort her. Even Mrs. Dressler, Adelaide, and Hannah spoke to her and tried to engage her in conversation not having to do with their current situation. One day, Mr. Dressler and Mr. Engelberg decided that it should be somewhat safe to try and book passage for the Engelberg family to Sweden.

CHAPTER 13

Captured!

Plans were made in secret with connections through the Resistance to get the Engelberg family on the next shipment through the fishing trade boats to Sweden. The plan was for Seth and Hannah to take the family into the woods to the halfway mark. There another group of two Resistance members would meet them and carry the Engelberg family over to the shipping yard at the coast and smuggle them into a fishing boat set for a long journey around Denmark to Sweden.

Adelaide was naturally disappointed she wasn't asked to come on the mission, but Seth assured her she would help with the next mission and that he and Hannah had this one under control. As the day approached, Adelaide insisted that something didn't feel right, and she pulled Hannah over to one side to speak privately. She began to plea with her, "Hannah, I have a really bad feeling about this. Something isn't right. We should stay in hiding for a few more days at least. The soldiers are on high alert."

Hannah felt Seth wouldn't risk their lives and she trusted his intuition, so she did not share the same feelings of hesitation that her friend now shared with her. Adelaide continued to plead with Hannah. When she realized it was pointless, she grabbed Hannah's hand and placed something in it just as the group was about to walk up the stairs to leave. Hannah felt what she thought was a string in her sweaty palm. She looked at Adelaide as they hugged. "Please, Hannah, be careful. This is a gift from me to you. You have been our

Brave Star. I am grateful to have met you and call you my true friend. I want you to have this gift. Follow the star, Hannah. It will always lead you home."

Hannah stuffed the string in her pocket and couldn't even speak other than to mutter between tears, "You too, Adelaide. I'll be brave for you."

They ascended the stairs and began to transport the Engelberg family for their voyage. The night air was cool, and Hannah calculated it was almost mid-April. Seth and Hannah made preparations and assisted Mr. and Mrs. Engelberg with their daughter, Amelia, out of the bookshop through the alley and out on to the streets of Amsterdam. They crept through the shadows to the woods. Everything went as planned. Once the group was safely in the woods, they could once again breathe easier. Almost to the checkpoint meeting place halfway through the woods, Hannah could hear the sound of dogs barking. Her adrenaline quickly kicked in and she began to quicken her pace. She used her finger to her lips to warn the young girl, Amelia, to not speak a word.

Just before the clearing where they were headed to meet the other Resistance members, two loud gunshots fired into the night. The group dropped to the ground in shock and to take cover. After a moment, they could hear soldiers yelling and dogs barking. Hannah knew in her heart that the Resistance group that had been waiting for them must have been discovered. She looked at Seth, and he had a look of anger in his eyes. They waited for several minutes before attempting to move. Just then, a hand reached out and grabbed Hannah. She spun to see a girl she knew to be in the Resistance. She whispered in her ear to get the Engelberg family to follow her, and she quietly led them away from Seth and Hannah.

The two teens sat low in the grass and trees waiting. They finally stood up without a word or sound made. Seth led Hannah to where the clearing was and there lay Peter, a Resistance member who had helped them with previous missions. He was dead. It was a gunshot wound to the chest. Hannah wanted to sob but didn't dare for fear that the soldiers were still close by, looking for more of the Resistance. The two turned and went back in the direction of

Amsterdam. As they moved further away from the whole scene, they silently prayed for the safety of the Engelberg family. When Seth felt they could whisper, he told Hannah his intention to go back later in the wee hours of the morning and bury Peter.

Just before they rounded the last wooded path before the edge of the woods, a soldier called out, "Halt!" Panic seized Hannah, and she froze next to Seth. They had been holding hands and continued to do so. Since Seth was in his blond wig, Hannah hoped they could pass for a couple out for a romantic jaunt in the woods after dark. She wasn't so sure though if that would be believable. The soldier glanced harshly at both teens and asked Seth, "Who are you, and why are you both out in the woods this late at night?"

Seth looked sternly back at the soldier. He said, "We are out for a moonlight walk. I am the son of a pig farmer, and she is my sweetheart. Why? Have we broken some law, Officer?"

The soldier glared at Hannah and she stared back blankly at him. He began to grab Hannah's other arm and spoke, "You are out past curfew. Where are your papers, miss?"

Hannah stared blankly at the officer. She didn't have papers. What papers?

Seth interrupted, "Here are mine, sir. I have her out with me. That should suffice."

The soldier glared at what Hannah assumed were fake Netherland identification papers and looked from Seth to Hannah. "I am going to need to take your girlfriend with me for questioning."

Seth became angry. "No, leave her alone this instant. You can't take her. You see, we will be in trouble if our parents all find out we have been out. We snuck out for a walk. Her parents will be furious if we don't get home before they notice she is gone. Please, let us go."

The soldier jeered at them, and grabbing Hannah more tightly, he and another soldier who had just appeared, began to drag her away from Seth.

"Ouch, stop! That hurts, let me go!" cried Hannah.

In one swift instant, Seth began to make a dart for them, and the other soldier hit Seth across the face and knocked him into a tree. He hit his head and lay motionless on the ground.

"No!" cried Hannah.

The soldiers laughed and dragged her away, leaving Seth alone and unconscious on the forest floor.

Hannah was terrified of these two soldiers, but she was more afraid for Seth. Was he dead? What would happen if he awoke and realized she was gone? What about the Dressler family? They would be expecting her back soon. She shook from fear and the chill in the damp night air. The soldiers led her to an office in what looked like a military headquarters. They roughly sat her down in a chair and told her to wait and not move. They locked the door on their way out.

Her adrenaline once again kicked in, and her brain went swiftly into overdrive. *Okay*, she thought. *I can be an American girl named Katie, who was traveling with my father on business. We just recently moved to Amsterdam and my mother joined us a month ago. I met Seth and we fell in love. He is my boyfriend and they have hurt him. If they don't release me this instant, then my parents will come looking for me, and it could cause an international crisis. There, that's believable, right?* She felt convinced of her story.

Just then a soldier and someone who looked like a general with many strange patches on his uniform sleeve, came into the room. "Keep calm, stop my heart from racing," Hannah pleaded with herself. She noticed as the men sat down at a desk that a strange-looking symbol hung on a red flag on the wall behind the desk. She had seen that black and white symbol before, she knew it was the Nazi symbol. *A swastika or something like that*, she thought.

The men faced her and didn't say a word. Finally, the general spoke to her, "We have had people smuggling and hiding Jews here in Amsterdam. You look a little Jewish, but also American. Who are you really and why are you here?" Hannah felt that panic in her throat and stomach and it made it difficult to speak.

Finally, she pulled her gaze away from their critical stares and found a small version of her voice. "I am Katie Smith. I am from America, but my parents and I live here in Amsterdam. We moved here for my dad's work. He is a doctor, you see." She stopped and wondered if she had gone too far.

"Are you a Jew?" he asked her harshly.

"No," Hannah answered honestly. "I am a Christian."

The soldiers stared icily at her. Just then, there was a disturbance outside the office door. Hannah heard what sounded like a muffled version of Seth's voice yelling out to her. "Katie! Katie, where are you? Your men have taken my girlfriend. Where is she?"

She had tears in her eyes and began to get up when the general spoke to her. "No! Sit there and don't move. It sounds like prince charming is here to defend your honor, princess," he sarcastically teased her.

Just then, another soldier knocked and entered with Seth standing in the doorway with handcuffs tightly around his wrists. "I'm so sorry, Seth. Are you hurt?" Hannah asked him through tears. She noticed a blood stain on his head where he hit it on the tree.

"Silence, you Christian American brat!" the general retorted at her pleas. Seth looked confused and stared at Hannah as though he had never seen her before. She let the tears continue to fall and slightly nodded her head at him as if answering the questions in his eyes. Yes, she was not only a Christian but also an American and would do anything or say anything to save their lives right now. He looked at her and finally gave her a slight smile. The soldiers then dragged him away out the door. She was alone again in the room and watched him go before falling back in her cold chair and let the sobs overtake her.

CHAPTER 14

Kamp Vught

Hannah assumed because she was American that she would be released and would make her way back to the little bookshop, but that would not be the case. She was left alone in that office for several hours and then roughly pushed from the room on to a train. She was so tired, hungry, and probably severely dehydrated due to exhaustion she did not put up a fight. She was loaded into a large smelly train car with maybe thirty other people. She realized these other people were Jews. It didn't take long to realize that they were being relocated, but she wasn't sure where she was. She admitted to the soldiers that she was an American, so why would they take her away from Amsterdam? She felt so tired that she gave in to her situation and sat down as the train car door was slammed, and within a few minutes, the rock and lull of the train made her give way to sleep.

When Hannah awoke, she was being forced out of the train car with the others out into the pouring rain. She didn't understand where she was or why this was happening to her. Had God not heard her prayer? She wanted more than anything to go home. She needed her parents, her little brother, and her warm bed. Would she ever see them again?

Hannah was ordered to report to the soldiers in charge at once. She knew without even being told that she was at a concentration camp. She saw a sign hung over the outside of an office building. The sign read, "Kamp Vught." She shivered as she stepped into a small cold office. The rain had soaked her from the inside out, and though there was a small fire in the corner of the office, she figured it was not for her use. A stern young officer asked her who she was and why she thought she had been brought here.

Hannah looked the man in the face and replied bravely, "My name is Katie Smith. I am an American who was caught in the woods with my boyfriend. I was forced to come here and I don't understand why. I do know when my father discovers I am missing, he will file for an international crisis to be announced." There she said it. She looked at the young officer who frowned deeply as she spoke.

He turned to some papers on his desk, and then without looking up at her, he asked, "So, where is your passport and papers?"

She hesitated slightly before responding, "At home. I snuck out of my house to meet my boyfriend who was also caught. He is from Amsterdam. I am from America. You see the complications with our families. I didn't bring my papers because I wasn't planning to be caught and treated this way." She defiantly concluded.

After a few moments, he responded, he looked up again at her and barked, "Well, well. What should we do with you then?" He asked more to himself than her. "I could make you work here as a cook or Jewish caregiver." He snickered at his own comment. Then he looked back at her cautiously. "You are sure you aren't a Jew?"

Hannah glared at him. "Of course not! I am an American who goes to a Protestant church. This is all a mistake. I would like to go home now, please," she pleaded with the officer.

"Home? How could I send you home now? You've seen our lovely accommodations and you don't want to stay?" he was taunting her slightly.

She stared at him and tears trickled from her eyes.

He looked for a brief second as though he had compassion on her. He began, "Look, you were brought here with Jews to be a member of our camp. We should find you lodging and put you to work. You will be treated with more respect and authority than a Jew, but a prisoner you are to be, nonetheless."

This could not be happening! She was a prisoner in a Jewish concentration camp? No!

She was escorted then by two other officers to a small building that was bare except for rows and rows of bunk cots lining both walls up and down. She couldn't adjust her eyes well to this dark, gloomy room. She found a dirty bed that was to be hers. A rat ran across the dirty floor beside her foot, but she barely flinched. The smell she thought came from there, she realized was from the furnaces and chambers. It made her stomach churn. She knew she would never forget that smell. Burning flesh has a specific odor you don't ever forget. It made her feel nauseated and like she would faint at any moment. The thought of people burning to death and dying from gas chambers was more than she could stand. She walked outside and, almost on cue, began to dry heave.

The food was a joke. *Slop* was the only descriptive word Hannah could think to call the blob of food that was put on her plate. She knew she should try and eat it, but she just couldn't get it to go down her throat. She gagged several times that day. She felt so weak and lonely. The other prisoners didn't speak at all. They were either afraid or so miserable they couldn't talk. She noticed that they all had been given numbers to wear on their uniforms, and she was still in her jeans and red sweater. She also felt the string in her pocket that Adelaide had given her before she left the night before. That felt like eternity since then. She went quietly to an outhouse and reached in her pocket to remove the string. She was alone in the stall and glancing at the gift, she saw Adelaide's Star of David necklace. She couldn't believe her eyes. Her friend had given her a most precious gift of faith to her. What was it she had said to Hannah that she was their Brave Star? "Follow the star, Hannah. It will lead you home." She didn't feel brave or like a star. She just felt hollow. Where was home anyway? She stuffed the necklace carefully inside her pocket once more and headed out to prepare for bed.

Her mattress was so rough she couldn't sleep. Finally, after hearing so many women and children in her bunkhouse crying themselves to sleep, she closed her eyes and prayed a heartfelt prayer to her Savior, "Lord, please help me. I know this can't really be happening. I don't understand why I am here. Is it to take the place of the Dressler family? I know they would have been sent here if they were caught hiding. Was I able to cause enough of a diversion to save them? Did they let Seth go? Is he okay? Oh, Seth, please be okay." Her thoughts raced. She began to softly cry into her hard mattress and before she knew it, she was asleep.

The next day, she woke up thinking she was living a nightmare. She was yelled at and pushed from her makeshift cot to be hustled to the chow hall. She was given a large spoon and put in the line to feed Jews in the camp. She was beyond exhausted and when another worker yelled at her to move faster, she almost threw back and slugged her.

Hannah began to pay attention to the Jews imprisoned in the camp. The men, women, and children were all separated from each other. Families were not allowed to be together. Small children were abandoned and treated as bad as adults. People were stamped and sent to different areas of the camp when they arrived from a train. Some were even sent immediately to the gas chambers. It broke her heart, and she spent hours every night crying for the lives lost. They must all work, even in the rain and mud. She had seen animals treated better than the way these Jews were treated.

Every morning on her walk to the kitchen for her work, she thought it felt like she was walking in snow, but in reality, it was ashes. Human ashes. One morning, she walked with a small girl who had big brown eyes and curly hair. The girl asked Hannah if she had seen her mother. Hannah's heart broke. She had no idea who this child was or who her mother was. It was devastating to be at this awful place. She realized she was there for a reason—to help others just as she had done in the Resistance. She thought about the missions in the Resistance and wondered if she had made a difference. Could she make a difference here in Kamp Vught?

CHAPTER 15

Escape Plan

One day, while she was walking back to her cabin, she noticed an opening in the fence on the back side of the camp. It wasn't a large opening but big enough to crawl through. She had a thought, "What if I could help people escape?" She thought she would ask several women in her bunk if they would know how to leave and run for freedom if they could get outside the fence. She asked one lady to get a feel for a response. The lady told her that if she were ever free, she would run till she reached a city and beg to be hidden. She also mentioned to Hannah that German soldiers were everywhere in the woods and that she knew she would never survive. It was a nice thought, right? Well, it was worth a try.

The little girl who walked with her, asking for her momma every morning, took to Hannah immediately. Hannah thought she reminded her of little Liesel. She was scared and alone. Hannah didn't understand the inhumane treatment of these people, and she made a silent oath to herself to help them. One day, the little girl was walking with Hannah and a soldier grabbed the little girl's arm. He dragged her off toward a gas chamber. Hannah screamed and began to run after them. "No! She didn't do anything wrong! Please, take me instead!" The soldier jeered at her and threw the little girl in a gas chamber. The look in the girl's eyes as she looked back at Hannah would haunt her forever. *That's it. I am done. I can't sit by and see this happening another minute. These people need to be set free. I will help them,* she thought.

Her plan seemed simple enough. In the days that followed, she had told fifteen Jewish women to wait until after final roll call checks in the morning after breakfast and to gather as many children as they could safely conceal. Then they were to sneak behind their bunk-house cabin. They were to wait for Hannah to give a signal that it was all clear and then to follow Hannah's lead to inch quietly through the opening in the fence. They were to rendezvous together in the woods and make their way the four miles to the nearest town. She believed some good citizen would take them in. If they were silent in the woods, they would not be caught by the soldiers in the woods.

Hannah felt a thrill as she realized she was single-handedly operating a covert mission in the concentration camp. If this worked, then others could also escape and be saved. She felt the Dressler family would be so proud if they could see her now, especially Seth. She couldn't think about him. She focused on the mission to take place after roll call that morning. She got up quickly and went to the chow hall kitchen. She mechanically went through the motions of serving breakfast to the Jews like normal. Everything was going as planned.

After breakfast, the Jews would always gather for morning roll call. They were separated by houses and assigned the day's duties or assignments. Some cleaned, others did manual labor, and some were sent to the gas chambers. No more lives would be lost on Hannah's watch. She made a vow to this. She would help them escape. She could do this.

As the roll call ended, she waited in the lavatory to not seem conspicuous. According to her calculations, this was the time that the soldiers would go in and have chow and coffee. She figured only two soldiers were on guard at the most on that side of the camp. The opening to the fence was blocked and she just knew this was the one opportunity to make the escape plan work. She didn't intend herself to go, because if this mission was successful, she would be able to help others do the same.

When the appropriate amount of time had passed, and she felt sure the soldiers were at chow, she crept out the side of the building and to the back. Adrenaline pumped through her veins. She knew this could be a disaster, but she had to try. She could not stand by and do nothing anymore. She had to help these people. The little girl's eyes looking at her from the gas chamber door made her even more determined to risk her life for these people.

Once she rounded the corner, she saw the Jewish women and children in place. No, it was too many. Maybe thirty to forty people. This wouldn't work, would it? She didn't expect this many and they only had a slim opportunity to escape while the soldiers on duty were on the other side of the building. Slowly, as if time stood still, the action unfolded.

The first set of five people were starting for the fence when the sickening sound of a soldier's command, "Halt! Stop there right now!" Three soldiers and a woman, who Hannah quickly realized betrayed the group by going to an officer to snitch, was standing there waiting for the Jews to try and escape. Hannah's heart sank. She stepped out from her hiding spot and immediately was seized by the soldiers. She was taken to the commander's office that she recalled she first came to when she entered the camp. He looked at her sternly. "Let me get this straight. You were attempting to rescue these people and help them escape!" he yelled at her angrily.

"Well, yes," was all she could say to him.

"How dare you! This is my camp, and no one escapes, not ever. You are a traitor and will be put to death!" he screamed at her, his face turning red.

"Death? Death is a gift in a place like this. You torture innocent people and treat them worse than animals. I wouldn't work another day in your so-called camp. I welcome death. This is a hole straight from Hell, and you will get the torture you inflict back on you seven-fold." Hannah calmly spit out at the angry leader standing before her. She would not cower down. She was not afraid anymore. The things she had seen and the torture others endured was more than she could stand another day of it.

"You are a smart-mouth little girl, aren't you? You think you are so brave I am sure, but remember, you did not save any lives today. You sent more people to the chamber. But you, no, you won't die that way. I have other plans for you. You will be publicly executed for your crimes. What good did your plan do you or them for that matter? You are a fool, young American." He spat out the words straight to her heart.

Hannah glared at him and unbelievably felt a sense of peace she had never experienced before. She didn't know how to explain it. She knew it must be the Holy Spirit calming her and reassuring her she was in His hands, not these German soldiers. She looked him straight in the eye then and said boldly, "You might as well kill me then. I will never stop fighting to free these innocent people from you. You are a monster just like your leader, and I will give these people hope until my last breath."

He grabbed her arm and walked her harshly to the courtyard area in the middle of the camp. Within minutes, people had been forced to gather to witness her execution. She was to be shot in the back of the head, as custom for traitors. She was surprised at how she wasn't afraid. She remembered the verse Mr. Dressler had said to the Kerns before leaving for Sweden. The verse described how God goes before her and will stand with her.

She thought of the Kerns and wondered if they made it safely to Sweden. She thought of the Engelberg family who were still at sea, no doubt. She thought about the Dressler family, and most importantly, her own family. Would they ever understand what happened to her? She knew she shouldn't worry about that. She was born to do this. She was made to help the people she had saved and give hope to those she hadn't been able to save. She knew she had made a difference and for that, she could die peacefully. She was then forced down to her knees on the cold asphalt.

The commander began to speak then, "This here is Katie Smith. She is an American Christian who was brought here for her illegal crimes. She has proven to be a little traitor and for that, she must be sentenced to death here today. Let her decisions be an example to you of how we treat traitors and conspirators here at Kamp Vught. We will now kill her to prove where your loyalties should lie."

Hannah sat on her knees with her hands bound behind her. She looked down at the asphalt and breathed a prayer. Just as she was about to be shot, one thought crossed her mind. Adelaide's voice came to her, "You are our Brave Star. Follow the star, Hannah. It will always lead you home." With her eyes and head lifted toward her Heavenly home, she smiled.

CHAPTER 16

Home

"Hannah, it is 10:30 p.m. Lights out, honey. You have school tomorrow. Did you finish your homework?"

Hannah jolted awake and squinted around the room. Home? She was home? She jumped up from her bed and hugged her dad tight. Tears flowed down her cheeks. "Oh, Dad. I missed you so much!"

Her mom stepped up behind them and looked concerned. "Hannah, are you okay, honey? Did you fall asleep in your novel again?" her mom asked.

Hannah quickly left her dad's embrace and hugged her mom. "Oh, Mom!" She sobbed into her mother's shoulder.

Her dad cleared his throat then. "Look, Hannah, I know I have been gone a lot lately for work. Your mom and I had a good talk tonight. We have decided to go to counseling together and maybe even plan a family vacation for next spring. How do you feel about Europe?"

Hannah laughed out loud joyfully. "Europe sounds awesome, Dad. Maybe we could go to Amsterdam or Germany. I would love to see a castle."

Her mom looked at her quizzically. "Germany, huh? Is all that history on the Holocaust you are reading for class making your brain a little fuzzy?"

Hannah smiled through her tears. "Maybe so, Mom. Maybe so."

Her parents kissed her good night and made her promise to change into her pajamas and turn off her lamp. As they left the room, she looked down and noticed she was still in her jeans and red sweater. Her denim jacket was gone, but she vaguely remembered taking it off in the hidden room one warm day and never put it back on after that. She absently reached into her pocket and pulled out the black string necklace and held it up in the light of the lamp. The Star of David shined in the light and her face broke out into a huge smile. *Impossible!* she thought as she stared at the necklace. It was a dream. She couldn't possibly have this necklace with her. With that puzzled thought in her mind, she changed clothes and fell asleep.

The next day in English class, she sat next to Riley. They were all handed a pop quiz, not much to anyone's surprise. What was a surprise was how well Hannah did on the quiz. She approached Mrs. Lannister after class and asked her if she could do an extra-credit project and presentation on the Holocaust to raise her overall grade average. She told her how fascinated she was with the topic and wanted to share her passion with others. Mrs. Lannister agreed she could do a presentation for extra credit the following Friday.

She spent the next week researching and fully engaged in her project. She used much of her own experiences to help her portray the Jews as a chosen people who were tortured for no reason at all, other than a man's pure hatred for a human race. She hoped she portrayed Hitler as the monster that he was and how his Nazi soldiers persecuted the Jews and made life difficult. She also focused on a life in hiding and how it was for the Jews. She even spoke of the concentration camps and how miserable they were. She felt like she had a good amount of content, but she worried she wouldn't be able to fully communicate her feelings and experiences in front of her class without looking like a blubbering idiot.

She asked Riley to help her do research. Riley had taken an interest in the Holocaust even before Hannah, and she felt she could use her friend's interest to pick her brain. Riley and Hannah found lots of great information, and Hannah felt confident in her research.

Occasionally, her mind wandered to the Dressler family. She wondered if they all were okay. Did Seth get released from the Nazi soldiers? They had no reason to question that he was a native Netherland boy who had made a mistake to sneak out at night for a girl. It was totally believable, but did he survive? What about the Dressler family? Little Gretchen and Liesel must be safe in their bookshop.

In her research, she searched and searched for their family and if they escaped the Nazis. Nothing was recorded about the Dressler family or their fate. This made Hannah feel unsettled. She wondered if everything was all for a loss. She knew it was a dream, but how did that explain the necklace? She couldn't explain to anyone where it came from. She knew to keep it tucked inside her shirt to avoid having to ask questions about it she wasn't prepared to honestly answer right now.

She often thought of her courage in the camp. She thought of all those Jewish lives lost and how if she had been more careful, would her mission have been successful? She also researched the camps, but found nothing that indicated any Jews ever escaped any of them. No record of it was found, which lead her to believe no one ever escaped the camps. Some were released after the fall of the German Nazi conquest, but no escapes. She spent hours pouring over books to find anything that even indicated that she had been there. Nothing. She found nothing.

Instead of becoming more frustrated about the lack of evidence that she was ever there, she began to make a case for the Jews that were there. She felt she could be their voice and help get their story out. She could use historical proof that these people suffered unimaginable things for the sake of Hitler's cause. She knew she could take their stories and bring them to life in her presentation.

CHAPTER 17

The Letters

When the following Friday came, and it was time for her presentation, she felt even more nervous than before. *What if they hate all the hard work I have poured into this? What if I sound like a complete flake? I may not get the point across.* She realized that thought made her feel she would let down her Jewish friends from long ago. She seemed sad all of a sudden. She wondered if she had made a big mistake and that she really was crazy and her lunacy would now be evident to everyone who knew her after this presentation.

"I can do this. I need to do this. Compared to everything she had been through in Amsterdam and the concentration camp, this was a cake walk, right?" She reminded herself as she sat down in her English class. Mrs. Lannister handed back their novel tests from the day before, and Hannah made an A. That made her feel a lot better about the whole presentation. She obviously learned things and knew what she was talking about, or she would have failed the test like the one she took a few weeks ago.

Mrs. Lannister called Hannah up to the front of the room. She brought a poster she had made full of pictures of Jews from the concentration camps she found online and a book she had found at the library. She also was wearing her Star of David necklace. She never took it off since the day she came home. She knew how important it was to wear it always. She took a deep breath and began her presentation. She felt confident she had everyone's attention as the details of the Holocaust unfolded in her presentation. By the end of it, some of her classmates were in tears, others sat looking sad, and some clapped for her.

Mrs. Lannister asked her to remain after class. *Uh-uh, what now?* She wondered. Mrs. Lannister congratulated her on the best presentation she had ever heard over the Holocaust. She explained how deeply it moved her to tears. She told her she was not sure what had inspired Hannah to take such a strong interest in the Holocaust, but she recommended several Holocaust museums for her to visit in the United States as well as Europe, and Hannah promised she would do that. She shared with Mrs. Lannister how her family was planning a trip to Europe for the next spring and how excited she was to tour castles and even concentration camps.

When she arrived home Friday afternoon from school, she stopped in the kitchen for a snack and to chat with her brother and mom. Beth would be coming home for the weekend, no doubt she needed to do her laundry, and Dad had bought tickets for the family to go see a college football game Saturday. It looked to be a great weekend. She had shared her new faith decision to accept Christ as Savior with her mom last week, the day after she came back. Her mom was happy she had made the decision. The family planned to attend church that Sunday.

She wanted to get a shower before supper, so she told her mom she would be in the shower and down in a bit to help with supper. As she was leaving the kitchen to head upstairs, her mom yelled to her, "Hannah, you had some mail come today. I left it on your bed."

Hannah responded, "Thanks, Mom." She didn't pay any attention to the letters on her bed. She quickly showered, dressed in her favorite sweats and T-shirt, and took off back down to the kitchen to help with dinner.

After a wonderful meal that included all of their family present, they all five played a few board games together. She beat her brother at Monopoly by snagging Park Place and Boardwalk. Mom gave them a run for their money when she quickly bought up three of the four railroad properties. Hannah almost hated to admit that she was glad her sister and brother were there and that everyone was happy. Mom and Dad were getting along much more, and he was home every day the past week by supper. She couldn't explain it, but that made her heart happy.

As she was headed off to bed, her mother asked her who the mail was from that she had placed on Hannah's bed. She said she forgot to check and explained it was probably one of the colleges she had requested information from or a company trying to sell her more cosmetics. She hugged her sister good night at the top of the landing and headed into her room.

As she shut her door, she turned on her lamp. She noticed the letters on her bed. She looked at the first one. It was postmarked with no return address, but the postmark checkpoint said Stockholm, Sweden. She sat staring at it for several minutes until her hands began to shake. "Sweden?" She didn't open it but looked at the other letter. It was postmarked from A. Dressler, Amsterdam, the Netherlands. A bubble of laughter rose up in her throat, and she had to stop herself short. "No way! It was just a dream," she said to herself. She absently shook her head and reached for the Star of David necklace around her neck and rubbed it back and forth with her left thumb. She sat in amazement as a smile crept across her lips.

The Mystery of the Letters

It had been three weeks since Hannah received the letters from the Dressler grandchildren. She could not believe that they had found her name and address in a book that had been among their parents and uncle's possessions. The letters were a thank you to Hannah for helping save their great-grandparents, mom, two aunts, and Uncle Seth from the Nazi soldiers. They assumed, of course, that she was an old lady by now. That was not the case, however. Hannah wondered how Adelaide's children were close to her age. She realized that continuing to question how the whole ordeal had been real would only drive her crazy. All she knew was that she thought she had fallen asleep in her history novel and woke up with a necklace she had not had before and a new understanding of how life was like during the Holocaust.

She wondered often about Adelaide, Seth, and the whole Dressler family. Did they survive? Of course, they did! They had children and grandchildren. Wow, she just couldn't believe it. If she didn't have the letters and the necklace, she would never have believed it herself. She kept her secrets to herself. She knew no one would believe her or understand her. Everyone just seemed to think she read a great book about the Holocaust and adapted a newfound respect for that time in history and the Jews who endured it.

Hannah, however, knew differently. Sometimes it was hard to keep her secrets to herself, but she knew she had to be the only one who knew. She had decided in the last few weeks that when she went to Europe in a few months with her family on vacation, she would go to as many concentration camps and museums as she could to learn more. She even felt God calling her to serve somehow. She wasn't sure yet in what capacity, but she knew she had found a passion for the Jewish people. She couldn't wait to go back over to Amsterdam and see things again. She planned to find that little bookshop she spent weeks hiding in and maybe even go see Kamp Vught. She wasn't sure how she could ever act normal when she got there, but she would try her best. She knew one thing for sure, she was a brave star who would shine her light to others in whatever way she could.

Shoes for Sarah

THE LOST STAR TRILOGY: BOOK TWO

Authors: Jessi Ratliff Lanier and Mary Ratliff

Hannah is back home from her family's trip to Europe and she still can't believe she and her best friend, Riley got to experience all the amazing castles, ancient cities and the concentration camps from The Holocaust. She will never forget her secret trip to Amsterdam that she experienced while she was able to help save many Jews from Hitler's soldiers. The adventure was dangerous, but she came back home to 2016 safe and in one piece.

Her adventures, however, are not yet over. She is on a new mission this time as she heads back in time to the Civil War. Only this time she isn't alone, a girl she knows from back home, Sarah, is there too! They are on a southern peach plantation and thrown into a totally new way of life they have never experienced before. Washing and ironing with no electricity, cooking over coal, and babies being born in a kitchen are just a few of the experiences facing her in 1863.

Last time she was stuck in the past her mission was clear, but what could she do this time in the middle of the Civil War 155 years before she was even born? When the soldiers and war come to the plantation will she be able to help these people and return to her home in 2018 before she gets hurt or even worse…killed?

Jessi Lanier is from a small town in deep East Texas. She grew up a preacher's daughter and the youngest of five siblings. Being a preacher's daughter prepared her for life as a pastor's wife as well. She is married to her husband of twelve years, and they have two young children. Jessi is a fifth-grade teacher at a small private school and has always been fascinated with the study of the Holocaust. She teaches various books and studies on the Holocaust in her reading and history classes and hopes to one day travel to Europe and see the concentration camps for herself. Her dream is to also visit a European castle and see the homes of Jane Austen and Charles Dickens.

Jessi has a degree in English and another one in nursing. She practices teaching, nursing, writing, works in ministry with her husband, and loves to educate others about essential oils. Her favorite books and inspiration are The Chronicles of Narnia and The Christy Miller series. She admires and looks up to many authors, but her favorites are Karen Kingsbury, C. S. Lewis, Jane Austen, Robin Jones Gunn, and Debra White Smith. She plans to continue to write in the transitional fiction genre with historical elements to her stories. Be on the lookout for her next book to come soon!